MEG EASTON

How to Not Fall for the Wrong Guy, Book Two in the How to Not Fall series

Copyright © 2020, 2025 by Meg Easton

Author website: www.megeaston.com

Also by Meg Easton

Romancing the Spy romantic comedies

Spies Don't Fall for Their Asset

Spies Don't Fall for Their Rival

Spies Don't Fall for Their Neighbor (coming 2025)

Spiced Chais and Secret Spies

Holiday Lights & Cocoa Cookie Nights

————

How to Not Fall romantic comedies

How to Not Fall for the Guy Next Door

How to Not Fall for the Wrong Guy

How to Not Fall for Your Best Friend

How to Not Fall for Your Ex

————

A Mountain Springs Christmas

The Christmas Pact

The Christmas Bet

The Christmas Clause

————

Nestled Hollow Romance

Coming Home to the Top of Main Street

Second Chance on the Corner of Main Street

Christmas at the End of Main Street

More than Friends in the Middle of Main Street

Love Again at the Heart of Main Street

More than Enemies on the Bridge of Main Street

———

Love Started romances

It Started with a Sunset

It Started with a Note

It Started with a Glance

———

Silver Leaf Falls romance

Coming Home to Silver Leaf Falls

HOW TO NOT FALL for the WRONG GUY

HOW TO NOT FALL for the WRONG GUY

MEG EASTON

Contents

1. Bex 1
2. Roman 12
3. Bex 26
4. Roman 41
5. Bex 46
6. Roman 52
7. Bex 62
8. Roman 77
9. Bex 87
10. Roman 94
11. Bex 107
12. Roman 119
13. Bex 130
14. Roman 141
15. Bex 155
16. Roman 168
17. Bex 179
18. Roman 188
19. Bex 196
20. Roman 200
21. Bex 204
22. Roman 211
23. Bex 218
24. Roman 228
Epilogue 231

Romancing the Spy 241
Missed any? 243
About Meg Easton 245

CHAPTER 1

Bex

I SIT BACK as my sisters Kenna, Nikki, and Roxanna talk over one another, discussing which pet is the one they would never let into their home—a mouse, fish, or a snake. My viewers love how lively the discussions get in my *Sterling Sisters* segments on my YouTube channel. I love it because everyone talking over one another is the sound of home.

A very lively, raucous, chaotic-as-a-crate-full-of-kittens home.

I turn to my oldest sister. "Let me get this straight, Kenna. You would seriously rather have a *snake* in your house than a *fish*? A fish can't even survive out of its tank!"

Sometimes, my sisters and I discuss serious issues, like politics, relationships, or world problems, and sometimes we discuss inconsequential or un-serious subjects, like which pet we don't want, where we'd go on a dream vacation, or our favorite fast food restaurant. It doesn't matter the subject

—all five Sterling sisters have reinforced-steel opinions and an even stronger need to share them.

"Yes, but," Kenna says, holding up a finger, "when I look at a snake, I'm not reminded of sixth grade, Joey Peterson, and how I accidentally killed the fish he gave me."

"Fair enough," I say. "I mean, as long as I don't have to ever have a bird in my house, I'm okay with whatever animal issues you all have."

"Asher wants a bird," Vivian says.

I throw my hands to my cheeks in horror. I'm partly playing it up for the camera but in reality, I do actually feel a bit of the horror. "You aren't going to let him, are you?"

"Are you kidding?" Vivian says. "Our house is already too much of a zoo."

"I forgot about you and birds," Nikki breathes, a mix of nostalgia and wonder in her voice. "It was because a couple of seagulls stole the bread off your sandwich at the beach that one time, right?"

"It wasn't *a couple*," I say, the hairs on my arms lifting just thinking about the terror of that moment again. Then I tell the story because my viewers love dramatic stories. Even if this one is my phobia origin story and makes me feel the drama myself. "There were *a dozen*. A dozen strong-winged, pointy-beaked, claw-footed swooping menaces. They didn't just steal my bread—it was my entire sandwich.

"And if stealing my lunch right out of my hands wasn't enough, then they attacked me! Even after I told them they could have my sandwich and ran away. They chased me down, stabbing their beaks into my pockets and squawking at me for being so rude as to not have brought more."

My sisters all give each other knowing looks, and Vivian holds up two fingers, mouthing *there were two birds* as if I can't see. I might be sporting an actual blush across my cheeks right now, but I'll take the razzing because my viewers are probably loving it.

"Whatever. You guys remember it how you want, and I'll remember it how it actually was." There were definitely a dozen of them. Probably more.

At the sound of ten kids bursting through the back door of the inn—which means they will be in the gathering room where we're filming in about 3.5 seconds—I say, "Thank you for joining us for a rousing Sterling Sisters segment. Don't forget to like the video and subscribe and—"

"And"—Fiona cuts in—"leave memes and gifs of birds for Bex in the comment section!"

"Don't do that," I say in my sternest voice, looking straight into the camera like I'm trying to bore straight into the thoughts of every single viewer. And knowing full well that my viewers are going to do exactly what Fiona asked them to do anyway.

I click the remote on the camera to turn it off as my four-year-old nephew, Drew, shoots through the room and leaps, plowing into his mom to give her a hug. I reach out to grab hold of the back of Vivian's chair and Nikki reaches out to do the same from the other side, keeping it from falling over backward from the force of Drew's hug.

"Woah," Vivian says. "You nearly knocked me over with that one."

"My love for you is strong," Drew says, pounding a fist into his chest.

"Make sure you save some for your siblings and your dad. Now run and get on your shoes—it's time to go."

"All the rest of you, too," Kenna calls out. "Shoes on and head to the lobby."

I stand, hold out a hand to my pregnant sister, Nikki, and pull her to her feet. Then I gather my sisters into a group hug. "You all are the best. Thank you, once again, for voicing your strong opinions, even when we disagree on things like the facts of certain events."

Fiona grins. "Oh, you love that we disagree, and you know it."

"True. These segments would be boring if you all didn't have such strong opinions that you'd defend with your dying breath, no matter how inconsequential the subject."

"I don't know about you all," Kenna says, trying to usher her three kids toward the front door, "but, Bex, I'll happily tell you that you're wrong any chance I get."

"As the one who has spent my entire life as the youngest in a houseful of bossy older sisters, believe me, *I already know.*"

My sisters shoo their kids toward the door while trying to gather up all their things and make sure every child has shoes on. Ten kids. And all I want to do is gather them together and surround them with hugs.

I don't know what look is on my face, but Nikki sees it. "You'll find the right guy soon. You'll add your own kids to the mix before you know it."

I let out a long breath. "I don't know—it's looking rather doubtful."

Once Kenna, Vivian, Roxanna, and all ten kids make it

out the door and into their cars, Nikki and I head back into the gathering room and to the desk I have set up near the back windows for our weekly planning session.

We sit across from each other and Nikki pulls out the planner that contains the schedule of my life, down to the minute. If it weren't for that planner, my life would be like a giant box of beads that burst open, spilling everywhere. That's why I hired her as my detail person—because Nikki takes care of all the little details that often get missed when I'm focusing on the big picture.

"The biggest thing we need to discuss," Nikki says as she absently rubs her hand on her pregnant belly, "is your plans for episodes that will go live during the judging period for the Eddie Awards."

I tap my pen on my lips. "For the *Sterling Sisters* segments, we need a couple of fun and interesting debate topics. Like what one non-electronic device you'd want if you were going to be trapped inside an office building for a month, or the most effective way to talk your significant other into choosing to watch the movie you want them to choose."

"Ha! I can already imagine Kenna's answer. Maybe we could even do one about our most embarrassing moments." She glances at her phone that just lit up, then picks it up from the desk. "Aww!" She turns the phone toward me. "How sweet is this?"

I lean in to see my brother-in-law's text that reads *This is what's waiting for you when you get home,* along with a selfie of him stirring a pan of chicken tikka masala.

"Is he the greatest, or what?"

"He's a solid four point five trillion times better than your last husband." I smile at my sister's pregnant belly—the belly that holds my future nephew—and I'm so glad that Nikki divorced the jerk before having any kids. I'm happy knowing that the little guy who's going to make an appearance in a couple of months is going to get such a good guy for a dad.

"You've got that right. Okay, so do you know what you're doing for the *Hidden Inn Roomies* segments?"

I nod. "Mostly. Still working out the details, but we'll have fun with that one."

"And your interviews?"

I grab Nikki's arm. "I can't believe I haven't told you already! I put a poll out to my viewers asking who they wanted me to interview, and I set it up so anyone could add choices to the list. As you can probably guess, the list grew to roughly the length of a CVS receipt in the first couple of hours, but then favorites started rising to the top. Guess who has been on top for the past thirty-six hours? Corbin Shields!"

"Are you kidding me?! Oh, wow, Bex. If you could get him…"

"I know. I want it to be a four-part interview, and I think he'd be so perfect for that. The guy has so much charisma, so many interests, and he's always willing to put on a show for his fans. If I could get him to agree to it, I think we'd have a good chance at this award."

"You'd have it in the bag. Getting him to agree to a four-part interview might be close to impossible, though."

"Even if he's willing, I'd have to hope his publicist could

fit it into the cracks of his schedule." It won't be easy, but I know the guy's fans are important to him, and so is appearing to be accessible to them. I think I can play up that angle with his publicist and talk him into it.

I grab my laptop that sits on the edge of the desk and pull it toward me, opening it and turning it on. "The last time I checked—which was over four hours ago—one hundred thirty-two thousand viewers voted to have me interview him. Voting closes in five days, and I'm hoping that he has an impressive enough number by then that he won't want to say no."

I log in and bring up the site. Then I just stare at the poll numbers, not comprehending what I'm seeing.

Nikki leans forward, squinting at the screen. "Who is Roman Powell?"

"*No.* No, no, no. How is he in first place?" I refresh the screen, hoping it's a mistake, but he's still in the number one spot. How did this happen? Corbin Shields is now in second place, a full nine thousand votes behind Roman. I run my hands over my face, but it's about as effective at reversing what happened to the votes in the past four hours as rewinding a movie in hopes that it'll end differently.

"Bex!" Nikki says. "Who is Roman Powell?"

"He's one of the groomsmen from Addison and Ian's wedding."

"Oh. The good-looking one who drove you nuts and made the flower girl chuck the flowers?"

"That's the one. Nikki, he can't win! Corbin Shields is so charismatic that not only will we be able to come up with some fun ideas for the interview, but my audience will eat it up. It'll be a win-win for both of us. Roman, though, is a cardboard cutout of a man in a tailored suit with a severe allergy to fun. His idea of an interview probably includes a desk, studio lighting, one camera angle, and zero smiles."

"But *who is he*? How do"—Nikki motions at the screen— "two hundred fourteen thousand of your viewers even know enough about him to vote for him?"

I shake my head. "I have no idea. Can we finish our planning session later? You've got chicken tikka masala and a sweet husband waiting for you at home, and I have some big questions for Ian about his groomsman."

As I say goodbye to my sister at the front door of the inn that my roommate Addison owns and runs as our apartment, sounds of chatting and smells of something delicious cooking come from the dining hall, so I head in that direction with my laptop.

All four of my roommates—Peyton, Timini, Addison, and Addison's brand-new husband, Ian—are all either behind the island counter cooking or sitting on the bar stools chatting. I breathe in deeply. "Is that shrimp scampi I smell? And here I was geared up for enchiladas or chicken piccata."

Addison grins at Ian as they stand side by side behind the stove. "It's one of Ian's specialties. And it's not the only fantastic meal he knows how to cook, so for our roommate dinners, we won't have to eat one of the only two I can make when it's my turn to cook."

I take a seat on one of the bar stools and place my laptop on the counter. "I knew it was a good idea to invite him to our roommate dinners."

"Because he *is* a roommate now," Peyton says.

"And I've enjoyed all four days of being one since we've been back from our honeymoon," Ian says and then gives Addison a kiss on her temple. "But I don't think I should come to every roommate dinner. Maybe every other time it should just be you four. The original roommates. Then on the weeks I come, it can be 'significant other' night or something."

"Except the rest of us don't have significant others," Timini says. "In fact, we made a pact not to." She raises an accusing eyebrow at Addison.

Addison holds up her hands. "In my defense, we made that pact when I had just come off a two-year relationship and before I realized that trying to resist Ian was pointless."

"And when Tim was still getting over her ex," I say, "and Pey had just stopped dating that guy who still shared an address with his mother, and I'd just gone on like my tenth date in a row with a guy who cried about his recent breakup." I lift a shoulder. "But none of us broke the pact."

"When you do, though," Addison says, "we will throw you an engagement party every bit as fun as the one you all threw for Ian and me. You're still planning on convincing Corbin Shields to let you interview him so he can fall in love with you, marry you, and be the father of your children, right?"

I can't believe I said that, regardless of how late we stayed up, or how punch-drunk we were from laughing during our roommate catch-up session last night. "That was the sleep deprivation talking. And besides, your friend," I say, jabbing a finger at Ian, "is putting my plan in jeopardy."

"*My* friend? Who? How?"

"Roman Powell." I bring my laptop back to life and then turn the screen toward Ian as everyone leans in to see it. "Any idea how in the world enough of my viewers even know who he is to have put him at the top of the list? Above Corbin Shields?"

Ian stares at the screen in confusion for a small moment, then looks up at the ceiling while whatever it is dawns on him. He chuckles, shaking his head. "Oh, wow. I can't believe that many people are voting for him." He takes a couple of steps closer and leans across the counter to get a better look at the laptop. "Whoa. He has two hundred eighteen thousand votes? What I wouldn't give to be in the room when he saw this. I wouldn't want to be the one to tell him, but man, would I love to see his face."

"*Why* is he on my list, Ian? He runs a small company that makes apps for phones. How do my viewers suddenly know who he is?"

Ian laughs, shakes his head, and then laughs again before going back to the stove to pour the shrimp scampi from the pan into a serving dish. "Before the wedding, he was hyped about an interview he'd had with *Business Success* magazine. They were going to feature ten stand-out CEOs, and they picked him.

"Then yesterday, he called. The magazine had released, and, well, it kind of pointed out that he was single and available and at the helm of a business that was going places. And they put him on the cover, looking a little..." Ian shrugs, "...like he was searching for someone to make him no longer single and available."

Addison puts her hand over her mouth like she's trying

to hold back a laugh. "Oh, my goodness. Oh, I bet he was mad. Can I please be in the room with you, honey, when he finds out about this poll?"

Peyton furrows her brow. "Why would that make him mad? I mean, he must've looked good and had a great article written about him if that many people want Bex to interview him. That's exciting and fun! Why would he not think it's a good thing?"

"You've met the guy," I say. "I don't think he does 'exciting and fun.' What was I thinking when I turned the interview choice over to my viewers? If I have to interview Roman, I'm as good as forfeiting my chance at the Eddie Award."

"I wouldn't worry about it," Timini says as she reaches out with a fork that seems to materialize from out of nowhere and sneaks a piece of shrimp from the serving dish. "It's just his fifteen minutes of fame. It'll be over in less than twenty-four hours, and Corbin Shields will make his way to the top of the list again."

"I hope you're right," I say. "Because I really want to win that vlogger award, and I can't do it with the wrong guy winning that poll."

CHAPTER 2

Roman

I LOOK DOWN at my tablet as I walk from my office to the conference room to meet with my department heads. In big, bold letters at the top of my meeting agenda is my company's and my own personal motto: *Be the Best You.* I like to remind myself of it before everything I do in my company.

But it doesn't pump me up the way it normally does. Probably because of the annoyed feeling that lately seems to always hang around like gum under a middle-schooler's desk, even when I'm not thinking about the reason why.

Four of my five department heads are already in the room. I glance at the empty seat. "Has anyone seen Everly?"

"I'm here, I'm here," Everly says as she blows into the room like a force of nature and slaps her stuff down onto the table before taking her seat. "Don't worry. I'm late for a reason."

"It's a good thing you're so skilled at what you do," I say, although we all know Everly isn't late. One of the things I love about my team is that they always show up five minutes early, ready to go. That, and they're all amazing at what they do and none of them complain about the slash in their job titles that means they are doing the work of more than one department. We're barely beyond startup status, and running lean is paramount. I've managed to bring together a dynamic bunch who all have the same goal as I do —to push the company forward.

Since this meeting is about the launch of our latest app, I start by going around the table and having each department head give an update on where they're at. The development department and the design and user experience department tell how things have gone for the advance users in the final round of testing, my finance guy talks about the advertising budget, and my assistant slash human resources head, Melinda, talks about a couple of promising interns we're about to give job offers to. The whole time, Everly leans forward, elbows on the table, tapping her pen or drumming a finger.

Melinda reaches out and puts a hand on top of Everly's fidgeting one but keeps her eyes on me. "The offers will go out today. Hopefully, they'll say yes because marketing and app testing could both really use the help." Then she looks at Everly. "With as much as you've apparently wanted to go first today, it wasn't the best day to come into the meeting last, was it?"

"No—I've been dying for my turn!"

Everly looks at me, so I motion to her. "Give us your

update, since it looks like you might explode if you have to wait another second."

Everly looks visibly relieved to finally be able to speak. "My team, of course, is always looking out for ways to have our products stand out in a crowded market. And an opportunity to help launch *Nudge Out* has practically dropped into our lap." She pulls a magazine from her stack and tosses it to the middle of the table, beaming.

And there it is. The source of the annoyed feeling that has followed me around since the magazine was released four days ago. I close my eyes, shaking my head, trying to keep my temperature from rising.

"Stop," Everly says. "You've got that vein by your temple popping out again. This is *Business Success* magazine! And you're on the cover! Remember how much we celebrated when you got the email saying they wanted to line up an interview and photo shoot with you because they chose you to be in their *Top Ten CEOs Under Thirty* list? And that was before they decided to put you on the cover. This is a big deal, Boss."

"It was a big deal back when I thought it would all focus on LivenUP and our products. It became considerably less outstanding when they changed the title of the feature to *Top 10 Young (and Single) CEOs* and chose a picture that makes me look like I'm smoldering at the camera."

I still don't know how they managed to snap the shot at all—I swear I didn't smolder at the camera a single time. It was probably taken at the moment when I suddenly wondered if I actually clicked send on the email I had written to Daran about setting up a meeting to discuss a new app idea. I can't help the fact that, with the right photographer, my thinking pose looks like an invitation to ogle me.

"It's a good smolder," Everly says.

"It looks more like they're advertising an episode of *The Bachelor* than spotlighting CEOs who have built successful businesses." The picture they used is a full-body shot of me in a suit, leaning against the back of a chair—a pose more suitable for a menswear model than a CEO. The second I saw it, I knew what my dad's reaction would be: embarrassment.

"But the article is good," Everly says. "They asked a lot of great questions about the company and our products, and you answered them perfectly."

I shake my head. "The article also includes a lot of personal stuff that I thought was just small talk. Off the record." It still makes me mad that I fell for it.

It doesn't matter what I say; Everly's excitement doesn't seem to dwindle. "But it shines you and this company in a great light. Pointing out that you're young and single doesn't take any of that away. What it *does* do is make people interested enough to want to find out more. And that's exactly the goal we had when you agreed to the interview. Who cares if they put you on the cover because you have a face that sells magazines? This extra exposure is golden."

"This is how I see it," Daran, my app development head, pipes in. "It's like you're going on a trip. You reserved a mid-sized car, but when you get to the car rental counter, they say they're out and they are going to upgrade you to an Aston Martin. Sure, it's only temporary. But it's an Aston Martin! Are you telling me you're just going to complain about how much gas it guzzles and not drive that beautiful piece of machinery every second you can?"

"This," I say, reaching for the magazine in the middle of the table and holding it up, "isn't an Aston Martin. It's not a gift. It makes me look like I'm not serious about this company. Or worse, that I'm not legitimate. That I only made the list because they needed someone to look good on the cover."

Sloan, my graphic designer slash user experience manager, crosses her arms and looks down, trying to hide a smile. With her looks and stature, she has probably dealt with the same thing herself more than once and is glad it's me this time.

"Whether you appreciate being on the cover or not," Everly says, "it *is* a gift. It's what got those investors you're meeting with today to be interested. They saw the 'shiny car' on the front cover and opened up the magazine to get the specs. It got their attention, just like it'll get the attention of others. It's a good thing, and we need to capitalize on it."

I fold my arms and lean back in my chair. I don't like it, but she has a point. It's enough that I should at least hear her out. "Tell me what you're thinking."

"There's a YouTuber who has a big audience, and she often does interviews with people. Six days ago, she put out a poll asking viewers who they would most like her to interview, and anyone could add a name to the list. The results were fairly predictable—various celebrities—until four days ago when *Business Success*'s latest issue came out. Shortly after it did, BuzzFeed picked up the online feature, and another YouTuber who makes videos also aimed at our target audience posted about it. Then someone wrote in your name as who they would like her to interview. Fast-forward four days and you currently have forty-two percent of *all* the votes. Nine percent more than the next most popular choice."

One of my biceps flexes involuntarily, and I raise an eyebrow. Forty-two percent. That's pretty impressive.

"My team has defined a very specific audience we believe it is vital to reach for the product launch of *Nudge Out*, and we've been brainstorming ways to reach that audience. We looked at the demographics of these viewers, and they are exactly the audience my team defined. An interview there might get people talking enough that it gives a significant boost."

"How big of an audience are we talking about?"

"She has over two million subscribers. Not all of them voted, of course, and she probably had a lot of people vote who haven't subscribed, but as of about five minutes before I walked in here, an interview with you currently has six hundred seventy-five thousand votes."

I sit up straight. That's a lot of people we could reach. "And you think we can get this interview?"

"If six hundred seventy-five thousand of my viewers wanted me to interview you, I don't think you'd have a hard time talking me into it."

"Okay, tell me about this YouTube channel."

Everly grins, probably sensing victory. "One of the things that I think definitely swings in our favor is that the creator is a woman who lives here in Oregon, so I think we'll get some extra hometown support." She pulls a manila folder from her stack of papers and slides it across the table to me. "Her viewers are rabidly loyal. She's no stranger to interviews, but she doesn't pimp products often, even for the people she has on her show. When she does, her fans jump at whatever she suggests, so if you can get her to suggest they use our app, it'll likely make a huge difference."

I open the folder to see a picture of the YouTuber, her opening screen logo, and her YouTube stats. I immediately shut the folder and push it back across the table toward Everly. "Yeah, this isn't going to work."

"What?" Everly says, looking around at everyone else, a bewildered expression on her face. "Why? Roman, this is *perfect.*"

I shake my head. "I met her a couple of weeks ago at my buddy's wedding—she's one of the bride's best friends. I know her and her channel well enough to know it's just fluff, and it's not the direction we need to go."

"Are you sure?" Wells, my finance guy, says. "It sounds like Everly found a potential advertising avenue that could have a great ROI."

Of course, Wells is focusing on the money aspects of it. One of the reasons why LivenUP is in such a great financial situation is because Wells guards our money like a mama bear guarding her cubs. Money isn't the only factor at play, though.

I hold up the magazine with my picture on it. "You want to capitalize on this, Everly? Great. There are some important things in this article. But there are also parts that are ridiculous and irrelevant. Those are exactly the same parts that Bex Sterling will try to capitalize on—*not* the important parts."

"I disagree. If she can get her Bexlandians on board, it'll be exactly the kind of boost we need."

I want to roll my eyes. *Bexlandians*. Not only would being interviewed by her embarrass my dad, but it's enough that even my brothers would get in on the ribbing.

"I think it would be a mistake to not jump on this," Everly continues. "Since you've already made a connection with Bex, it would probably be best if you reached out, but if you'd prefer, I am happy to as well."

With as happy and energetic as Everly is, she often gives the impression that she's easygoing. But she doesn't back down when she sets her mind to something. It's one of the reasons why I hired her and why she's a department head. But I'm still the boss, which means the decision rests with me.

"No. Don't contact her." I feel my phone buzz in my pocket and pull it out to see that it's my dad calling. Probably about my meeting with the potential investors. Since we've already discussed everything here that we need to discuss, I might as well answer my dad's call now instead of dealing with him later.

"But—"

"Everly, it's a firm no. Thank you all for your input this morning. Meeting adjourned."

As I walk out of the room, tablet in hand, I answer the phone. "Hello?"

"Hi, son. Today's the big day, right?"

"It is." I head down the hallway toward my office.

"And you've got a spit-shine on your business plan?"

"It's all ready to go. I meet with them in thirty minutes." Of course, it's all ready to go. These investors could mean the difference between LivenUP moving forward slowly and really becoming a major player in the app world. Everything I've been doing—everything I've helped this company to do—has been with investors in mind. Their support could mean everything.

"Okay, listen up. You may sell some apps that they might consider 'entertainment,' but you're a serious businessman. Show that to the investors. Don't fall for the same tricks that the interviewer at *Business Success* used on you. You're young and don't have a ton of experience with the media yet, so you didn't know how sneaky they could be. I don't blame you for the article turning out the way it did. But 'fool me once' and all that. Fall for it again, and it's on you."

I grind my teeth at the young and inexperienced comment but keep my mouth shut. My dad is probably sitting in his office behind his massive mahogany desk, floor-to-ceiling windows behind him. He might be leaning back in his chair, looking relaxed, but the man is a boulder the size of a house and impossible to so much as budge. This man would hate every single thing about me being inter-viewed by Bex Sterling.

When I get back to my office, I set the tablet on my desk and start flipping through the pages in the first of four manila folders, checking to make sure I have everything.

"Keep things professional with these investors. If they start asking personal questions, steer it away. Show them you can keep your eye on the ball. And son?"

"Yeah?"

"Land these investors, and we might just have to cele-brate by going on a rafting trip down the Columbia."

I'm so speechless I can't respond. My two younger brothers have each made our dad proud enough to earn a trip down the Columbia—Drake when he was interviewed for a business magazine after landing his first Fortune 500 company as a client, and Legend when he sold his first archi-tectural design—but it's been quite a while since I had anything on the horizon that my dad deemed worthy enough to even dangle the carrot. Nothing is going to stop me now from doing whatever it takes to get these investors on board.

"Now head into that meeting and show them what a Powell is made of!"

"I will. Thanks, Dad."

———

I successfully shake off all talk of the *Business Success* article and walk into the meeting with the investors feeling calm, confident, and ready to convince them to invest in LivenUP. My presentation is professional, precise, thorough, and concise. If my dad were a fly on the wall, he would be flying over to give me a pat on the back.

When I finish, the investors talk a lot about their vision of the company, which mirrors mine, and how they don't want to interfere with the way I run my business. If they had wanted to control how I run the company, I would've walked away. They ask lots of questions, and I field them left and right, the consummate professional. I ask them questions, too.

Then, Thomas Hayes, the investor who seems to be in charge, closes his folder and places his hands on top of it. The other two follow his lead, and then they all look at each other and shift in their seats. "You've built a good company here. I can tell you've put together a solid team of people, and that you're all working together for the same goal."

I nod. That's exactly how I feel about LivenUP, so I'm glad they see it, too. I hold my breath for the *but*, though. So far, everything is too good to be true.

"But we knew all that before coming here today. We've had our eye on you for months exactly because of all the things you just confirmed for us. We didn't ask to meet until now, though, because we were waiting to see the spark. That extra something that would tell us that you were going to be around for a while and that you were going places. We saw that spark in your interview in *Business Success*."

I flinch in surprise. What could they have possibly read in that interview that made them want to invest more than the presentation I just gave?

The woman sitting next to him adds, "We didn't really see that spark today."

How could they have not seen a spark today? I love this company, and I know that I've spoken about it with a lot of passion. Sure, I don't let them see *all* the passion I have—that's part of being professional, after all—but they had to have sensed it.

The third guy leans forward, resting his arms on the conference table and meeting my eyes. "Too many CEOs keep their noses to the corporate grindstone and lose touch with the customers that they are creating products for. We want to see that you are keeping that connection to your users."

"Keeping in touch with the pulse of our users is something we take very seriously here," I assure him. "We have a user experience team who tries out new ideas with focus groups, works closely with beta testers, polls our audience for preferences, and implements all the feedback we get. It's one of the reasons why our apps are rated so highly in app stores."

"And that's important," the woman says. "We wouldn't be here if you didn't do all those things. But that's not the spark we're talking about. That's how you connect to your audience. We are talking about how your audience connects to *you*."

"Why does that matter? I'm the man behind the curtain. I'm supposed to be invisible."

"Once upon a time, sure. And for most types of businesses, it still very much is. But not for a company like yours, and not if you want to grow in the way that we think our investment will help you grow. It's time for you to come out from behind the curtain. Your audience needs to see you and be able to connect with you. They need to view you as a real person. Find a way to do that, and we'll have no problem investing in LivenUP."

They get up to leave, so I walk to the door to see them out, feeling baffled. I'm not sure I really understand what they expect from me. As the woman reaches the doorway, she pauses and says, "You wear your professionalism like a mask. We want to see the man behind the mask. The part of the interview where you said you eat oatmeal every morning with peanut butter and jelly in it was a nice touch. Keep up stuff like that, and you'll do great."

The part of the interview that was supposed to be off the record and had absolutely nothing at all to do with my business—*that's* the part the investors liked? How am I supposed to remain professional yet "connect" with my users like that? They've given me a proposal about what they can do for me, and I really want them to invest. But I'm not sure I can do what they're asking.

I walk them to the front door and stand there long after they leave. I couldn't have asked for investors who are more on board with the direction I'm taking my company. With their backing, I would be able to grow the company the way I've been envisioning for so long but haven't been able to do yet.

And signing with them would make my dad rafting-trip proud. But signing with them also means doing something that would make my dad the opposite of proud.

I'm not thrilled about it myself, either.

And I know that I shouldn't care what my dad thinks, but I do.

Everly comes up to me and stares out through the glass doors with me for a few moments before asking, "How did the meeting go?"

"What do you think the chances are that my dad would watch *Bexlandia*?"

Everly snickers and I look over at her.

"Sorry. What do I think the chances are that Dr. Richmond Powell IV, D.B.A. will watch *Bexlandia*? Zero, Roman. I think the chances are zero percent."

I really hope she's right. I nod, my mind made up. "I think I'll reach out to Bex Sterling."

The smile on Everly's face isn't visible from where I stand, but I know it's there.

CHAPTER 3

Bex

When my thirteen-year-old nephew, Enoch, kicks the ball, I run from third base toward home. Dylan catches it, though, and quickly throws it at me. In an attempt to keep it from tagging me, I dive, landing in the grass of my parents' backyard a good foot away from home base. And the ball hits me anyway.

I don't even have time to push myself up before three of my nieces and nephews pile on top of me, pinning me to the grass.

"Guys," I say, laughing, "this isn't football!"

My seven-year-old niece, Tessa, leaps onto us, adding to our pile of bodies. "No, but our parents said we get bonus points for tackles anyway."

I manage to free my arms so I can tickle my niece. "But you're on my team!"

"And you're supposed to be on second base," Asher says. Then he pushes off me and races after the kickball.

"Dinner's ready," my dad calls out from his station in front of the barbecue, and the score and where everyone is supposed to be is forgotten.

I'm at the food tables with the rest of my sisters, brothers-in-law, parents, and everyone's kids, putting items on my plate, when my phone buzzes. I pull it out to see it's a text from Ian, my newest roommate.

> Ian: Remember how you asked about Roman Powell the other day?

> He wants to meet with you and is hoping to set up a dinner with you through me. He wants Addison and me to come, too, probably to make it less awkward.

> What should I tell him?

I turn my phone so that Nikki can see it.

"Wow. Roman is coming to *you*. I assume he's planning to ask for an interview. Are you going to say yes?"

"Of course, I'm going to try to make an interview work! Voting closes in two hours, and he's got nearly *half* of all the votes. As much as I wanted to interview Corbin Shields, Roman has two hundred thousand more than him. Roman Powell is who my viewers want to see. I was going to contact him as soon as the barbecue was over, but it looks like now I won't have to." I type out *Tell him yes* one-handed and slide my phone back into my pocket.

I'm just putting a big scoop of potato salad on my plate when my five-year-old niece Chelle tugs on my shirt. "Aunt

Bex? Do you have a corner brownie? Because I called one, but Drew took the last one and then licked it."

"I do have one. And because I think you're the bee's knees, I'm giving it to you." Chelle beams as I put it on her plate.

Nikki shakes her head. "You're such a pushover."

"Nope—it's all in service of my goal. Maintaining 'Favorite Aunt' status with the kind of competition we have isn't easy, so I have to butter them up any chance I get."

"I really need to step up my game," Nikki says as she reaches across the table to grab a roll. "What's your plan if an interview with Roman doesn't work out?"

"Then we sweet-talk Corbin Shields's publicist. My readers would be sad I couldn't get Roman, but Corbin would make for a much better interview. I'm pretty sure they wouldn't mind that for a consolation prize if I at least tried to get Roman first."

"And it might just win you that Eddie Award."

———

I step into the lobby of the restaurant with Addison and Ian. Ian set everything up with Roman, and he said Roman was the one who chose to travel from Gresham to Quicksand. Okay, so maybe the guy gets a checkmark in the positive column for that one. I don't know if it was Ian or Roman who chose Buffalo Bill's Steakhouse—not that there are a ton of other choices in Quicksand.

We check in with the hostess, who says, "Oh, I've already seated the other rough rider in your group."

Wow. He's early, even. Another checkmark in the positive column. As the hostess leads us across the Western frontier-inspired decor, complete with lassos, horseshoes, wanted posters, wagon wheels, and saddles attached to the walls, Roman stands up from our table at the far end of the room. He's dressed in a suit, which seems at odds with the cowboy hat light that is hanging just above our table and the boot-shaped menu holder on the table, but to each his own.

Overdressed or not, the man looks stand-up-and-applaud fine in a suit. Like millions of others who wouldn't normally pick up an issue of *Business Success* magazine, I've seen him on the cover. They made a good choice in putting him there—I heard it skyrocketed their sales. If I can just get the guy to let his guard down a bit and stop being so stiff and serious, an interview with him might do really well on my channel.

When we reach Roman, he greets Ian and Addison, and the two take their seats at the table—thankfully across from each other—and Roman holds out a hand to shake mine. And wow, it's a good handshake. It sends zings of electricity right up my arm. I had put my arm in his as we walked up the aisle together as a bridesmaid and a groomsman, but I haven't touched his hand before.

"It's good to see you again, Bex."

"You, too," I say as we both take our seats across from each other. "Started any brawls between three-year-olds late-ly?" I don't know why I say it. Probably to try to crack that shell of seriousness just a bit.

But Roman's brows knit together, and I can practically see his defenses rising. "I wasn't the one who—"

"Either way," Addison interrupts, "it was a fun moment to catch on camera. Made the wedding even more memorable."

Then she shoots me a look, so I put on my best innocent yet apologetic expression.

As we each give Roman our recommendations on the menu, I study him. When I look at him through the lens of my viewers, I notice how much depth his beautiful brown eyes have. As if dark chocolate, milk chocolate, and honey all tried to see how epic they could be if they formed a team. His skin has a golden glow to it like maybe he doesn't spend all day scowling at a computer screen.

And that jawline, too. The first time I saw him, I immediately wanted to put my hands on his face and feel that perfect amount of scruff. To run my fingers through the hair just above his ears that curls slightly.

Of course, that was back then before I'd spent some time around him. But I'm sure my viewers will be noticing that fine jaw and everything else I noticed my first time seeing him.

The waiter comes over to take our order. He's probably twenty-one but looks seventeen or eighteen and introduces himself as Kenyon, which I already know from eating here so often. When I order the sirloin steak and baked sweet potato, from the corner of my eye I see Roman's flinch of surprise, so I look over at him. "What?"

"I'm impressed you got the steak."

I lift a shoulder. "This is a steakhouse. 'When in Rome' and all that."

He nods, and then also orders a sirloin steak, but unlike

the rest of us, he orders a regular baked potato. I think about telling him that their sweet potatoes are to die for, but I let it go.

After the waiter leaves, Roman asks Ian and Addison how their honeymoon in San José del Cabo was, and they both light up like a grandma who was just asked to show off pictures of her grandkids.

I'm glad the two of them are sitting across the table from each other. Not only does it mean that Roman and I can discuss business face to face instead of shoulder to shoulder, but it means that Ian and Addison can only make moon eyes at each other instead of cuddling up, basking in their honeymoon glow, making things awkward for Roman and me.

But man, do I wish Roman would relax a bit. Slouch in his posture. Be a little less guarded. Maybe ditch the tie and undo the top button. I'm wearing a dress, but a casual, wear-grocery-shopping-on-a-Tuesday dress. And, because we're at Buffalo Bill's, I'm also wearing cowboy boots. Addison and Ian are both wearing jeans.

It's not that I have anything against seriousness. My dad is rather stoic, and I love him. He's a pretty cool guy. But on Roman, it feels wrong. I read people pretty well, and with Roman, it feels like the inside doesn't match the outside. That there's more to him than meets the eye.

Kenyon returns, holding a tray with our drinks on it, and starts passing them out. "Okay, and you two also wanted water on the side, right?"

Roman and I both nod, so the waiter puts one in front of me. As he's reaching out to place Roman's water in front of him, Cassie, one of the other waiters, turns around from a table she's waiting on and bumps into Kenyon's back. As Kenyon lurches forward, the glass of water spills all over the table and onto Roman.

"Oh, no. I am so sorry, sir." He pulls some napkins out of the front of his apron and starts dabbing at the water. "I am so sorry. I didn't mean to…" He holds out a few napkins, like he's going to press them against the water that has spilled on Roman's suit, but then thinks better of it. Good choice.

"It's okay," Roman says. "We'll just go with the flow. It's all water under the table now."

Huh. It's almost like there's a real person under the exterior he always has up.

Roman didn't come into town much before the wedding, so I haven't gotten to know him too well. Mostly what I know is that he was even serious at a wedding and that he thought he knew much more about kids than me. As the outcome of the flower girls walking down the aisle showed, he clearly did not.

Something catches my eye, and I glance at one of the tables to the side of us. It's a family of four, and the two daughters, who look like they're maybe ten and twelve years old, are looking at us, giggling and trying to nudge each other out of their chairs. They both seem to get nudged enough at the same time because they stand up, shoot a glance back at their parents, and then timidly walk over to our table, bumping each other the entire way. They're probably fans. I'm not recognized everywhere I go, but things like this happen about once a week or so.

The girls don't come up to me, though—they go straight

to Roman. The older one taps the younger one twice on her shoulder, but the younger one whispers, "No, you ask him."

So the older one stands taller and says, "Um, we were just wondering, are you Roman Powell?"

Roman's head cocks ever so slightly, showing his surprise that two girls he's never seen before know his name. "Yes."

Both girls giggle, but the younger one says, "We read about you."

Roman's eyebrows shoot right up. "You did?"

The older one nods. "And from the way you're sitting, your pants come up just a bit, so we saw that you're wearing fun socks, just like you said you did in your interview. We wanted to tell you that we think it's cool."

"Yeah," the younger says, "and I wanted to tell you that Emma has quoted your phrase 'Life's too serious for your socks to be' like five million times."

He doesn't say anything for a long moment—he just looks back and forth between the girls. Then, finally, he manages to get out, "You read *Business Success* magazine?"

"Well," the older one says, "it's our mom's, but I saw you on the cover—"

"*I* saw you on the cover," the younger one corrects. "And so I showed my sister, and then we read the article together."

"Well, okay, Bailey saw it first. But I made a goal to someday be on the cover of *Business Success*, too, because I'm going to start my own business."

Roman smiles a big, genuine smile. "That's a great goal. I hope you do."

The girl beams, but then her younger sister says, "I think

she just wants to be on it because she has the magazine with you on it hiding in her room so she can make kissy faces at it every night. If she gets on the cover, then it can be right next to your cover and the two magazines can basically get married."

"Bailey!" the older sister hisses. "I can't believe you just told him that!"

The girl shrugs, hands upturned. "Well, Dad says to always tell the truth, so…"

Red-faced and humiliated, the older girl turns her back on her sister and stomps back to their table. Bailey shares a faux innocent smile with Roman, then whispers, "She's going to be mad at me for like a week, but it was totally worth it."

Roman looks about as horrified at the exchange as the older sister is, and I try really hard to hold in my chuckle. I'm used to conversations like that with young fans, but Roman obviously isn't. If anything, it shows that audiences can really connect to him. They don't connect with everyone —I hope he realizes what a gift that is.

"Aww," Addison says when she turns back from seeing the girls sit back down at their table. "Your fans love you."

"They weren't—" Roman says. "They aren't even *Business Success's* target audience."

Our conversation is halted as Kenyon comes over to our table, carrying a much bigger tray with our food on it, and puts the stand into place in the aisle. As he's lowering the tray to the stand, Callie bumps into him again, and exactly one plate slides off the tray and onto the floor: Roman's. The one with the regular baked potato.

A quiet, frustrated growl comes from Roman as Kenyon stands frozen for a long couple of seconds. Then Roman mutters, "Do they not teach you how to share the aisle here?"

Kenyon scrambles to the other side of the tray stand and picks up Roman's plate, putting the steak, baked potato, and steamed veggies back on it. "I can't believe this is happening. I'll get them to make you a new meal." Then he holds Roman's plate, twisting side to side like he's just realized that he has nowhere to put the plate while he serves the other three plates of food.

I feel awful for the kid. It's bad enough to deal with an issue like that without the comment Roman made. I reach out and put a hand on the server's arm. "It's okay, Kenyon. It wasn't your fault. Why don't you take that to the kitchen, and do you mind bringing back an extra plate when you come?"

As Kenyon races off, I look at Roman and take a deep breath. "Do you have siblings?"

He jerks back a little at the abrupt change in subject. "Yeah, two brothers."

"Did you do things to annoy each other growing up?"

He nods. "Like it was a sport."

"Where are you in your family?"

"Oldest."

"So when other people picked on your younger brothers, what did you do? Join in like it was a sport?"

"What? No. I stepped in and said that if they messed with my brother, they messed with me."

I nod. "This is our restaurant. It's family. Don't mess with it."

I could swear a smile tries to break its way through to Roman's face. Then he meets my eyes and says, "I want you to interview me."

Kenyon comes back and places the empty plate near me, then gives Addison, Ian, and me our food. He opens his mouth like he's going to apologize to Roman again, but Roman beats him to it.

"I apologize for what I said earlier. That was very unprofessional of me."

Unprofessional. He's not apologizing for being a jerk, but for being unprofessional.

As I cut my steak and potato both in half and move half of them and my steamed veggies to the empty plate, I say, "So, I point out that you were rude, and you respond by asking me to interview you?"

"You don't have to give me half your food. They're remaking mine."

I push the plate across the table to him. "And I expect you to share with me when it gets here." Then I keep my eyes on him, one eyebrow raised, waiting for his response.

"My last interviewer was very accommodating and would've never told me off. I didn't like that interview much." He takes in a slow breath. "So here's the thing. I saw your poll asking who your audience thought you should interview. By a strange twist of fate that I don't think either of us would've guessed a week ago, my name is at the top of that list. My company is launching a new product, and my social media manager thinks our audiences overlap. And I figure that you want to give your viewers what they want. So, if we do an interview, we both win."

I take a bite of potato and chew slowly. I have a big audience—Roman would be stupid to not want the interview. But I have imagined how this meeting would go many times over the past few days, and it always ends with him not saying yes to it. Truthfully, it surprises me to hear the words that he wants the interview actually coming out of his mouth.

"Okay, then, let's talk." My usual strategy is to ease my way into what I want, but that doesn't feel right with Roman. I sense he likes things straightforward and blunt. "I want a four-part interview."

"No. We can cover it in one."

"I don't—"

"If we're only talking about me and my company, one is sufficient."

I study him long enough that I hope I make him uncomfortable. I don't like being cut off or having someone else tell me how to run my own show. "I'm not CNN, and this isn't a news story. People go to my YouTube channel because they want to be entertained. I am successful because I know what they want, and I give it to them. If you want this interview, it'll be in four parts, and each one will be in a different location so it won't get boring."

"Do your viewers get bored easily?" I'm thinking of all the witty jabs I could make, but he must sense them coming and doesn't want to take the insults, because he adds, "If you'd like me to do demonstrations of my apps, we can do it in four."

"The interview won't be only about your company and your apps. And we aren't just going to talk about the surface stuff when we talk about you and your company. Oh, now stop looking so panicked—I'm a good interviewer. You'll have fun. It won't be nearly as uncomfortable as whatever it is that you're imagining right now."

I think I'm lightening things up, but whatever stoic wall he's built, it's strong.

He starts sawing his steak into bite-sized pieces like he's pouring all his frustration into it. Honestly, I worry about the knife. And the steak. And the plate. "How comfortable I am during the interview isn't the issue. It's that people don't need to know about the personal stuff. It's none of their business. I just want them to get interested in my business and our products."

I jab at a zucchini on my plate with my fork and meet his eyes. "You're looking at this wrong. If they get interested in *you*, they'll be interested in your business. I read your *Business Success* interview, and I can see why people are eating it up. That pretty face on the cover got them to open the magazine to read about you. But it was things like the fact that you wear fun socks because it's the one way you can express yourself and still dress professionally that got all my readers interested in you and dying to know more about your business."

Roman narrows his eyes. "Nobody needs to know about what kinds of socks I'm wearing. Did you not see how awkward having that information out there makes things?"

"Did you not see how invested in you those two kids were? And the interviews are not going to only be about your socks. They're just not going to only be about your business or your products, either."

"It doesn't need to be about any personal things at all! I'm not looking to be a celebrity. I don't need people to get to know me or to like me—I just want them to enjoy our apps."

"And I think you're wrong." I look at Ian and Addison for help in explaining to this bull-headed man why it's beneficial for him to open up a little. It doesn't even have to be a lot—I'm not asking him to divulge his secret hopes and fears. All it has to be is a few bits for my readers to connect with him. But the two of them look all too happy to be staying out of the fight.

Why am I pushing for this so much? Just so I can win? To claim that I'm right? I don't even want to do this four-part interview with him. "Do you know what? No, you're right. If you don't want people to get to know you or like you, then my channel really isn't a good match, regardless of what my viewers think. You should be on a show that better fits with your goals—one where they only talk about businesses and products."

"And you should stick with interviewing people like… Who was in second place again? Some movie star?"

Kenyon comes over just then, holding Roman's new plate, looking like he has just stepped into a field of mines and isn't quite sure if he dares take the half-step closer to our table to set down the plate. He does, though, then quickly steps back. He opens his mouth to say something—probably to apologize again—but Roman speaks before he gets the chance.

Without taking his eyes off me, he says, "Actually, do you

mind boxing this up for my table-mate here? I'm sure she's going to need a good solid meal before her next interview because her viewers are dying to know what kind of socks Corbin Shields wears."

"And I'm sure that Corbin Shields will see the value in letting them in on a minuscule part of his life."

"It sounds like it's an interview match made in heaven." Roman pulls out his wallet, opens it, takes out several bills, and then hands them to Kenyon. "This should cover all four of us. Thank you for your service—keep whatever is left as a tip." He turns to his right. "Ian, Addison, it's good to see you again. Bex, thank you for meeting with me." Then he stands up and walks away in his overly-fancy suit, looking like a dream.

I watch him until he exits the lobby doors at the other end of the building because if nothing else, he does look mighty fine in that suit. Then I pull his plate—the one that contains the other half of my meal—toward me. "On the bright side, I got dinner with two of my favorite people, and I got half of my steak cut up for me." I stab a piece of it with my fork and stick it in my mouth, enjoying every bit of the perfectly cooked morsel.

I should be mad right now. Or at least frustrated. Why do I feel so exhilarated? Probably because I actually got to defend what I do to someone who sparred back and held his ground. Even if he did duck out before the match was over.

CHAPTER 4
Roman

I'VE BEEN DREADING my eleven o'clock meeting with Everly since I came into work. I know what she's going to say, so I schedule the meeting to take place in my office instead of in the conference room or her office, just so I have home-field advantage. It's a jerk move I usually don't use on my own employees, especially on my inner team, but desperate times.

My office door is open and she blows in like the north wind, not even waiting until she's fully seated or has put her tablet down before she asks, "So, how'd your dinner with Bex Sterling go?

Unwelcome as it is, my mind fills—once again—with all the emotions from last night. The water spilling on my lap. The waiter dropping my food and my reaction. Embarrassment at the two sisters talking about my article. How amazing Bex looked in that dress and cowboy boots. How infuriating it is that the woman can't agree to do a simple interview.

"Not well. There won't be an interview. So let's go over the plans we have in place for the product launch and brainstorm ways we can get it where we need to be."

"Wait. Why? What happened? Did she just say she didn't want to? After so many of her viewers requested you?"

I let out a frustrated breath that Everly won't just let this go. Not that I thought she would, but it sure would make things easier. "We both agreed that it wasn't a good match. End of story."

"But it *is* a good match! Did she give you a hard no? Because I don't think we should let that stop us from trying again. I bet I could smooth things over with her."

"Everly. The interview—which would be four parts filmed at four different times, by the way—isn't going to work out. This meeting is about finding other options. We need to turn our focus to that."

Everly leans back in her chair—something she so rarely does that its piercing effect feels stronger. Especially because she also crosses her arms, studying me. She stays silent for a long moment before she says, "Remember shortly after you hired me when you formed your inner team? In that first meeting with Daran, Sloan, Melinda, Wells, and me—all of us together—you said that we need to respect your decisions."

"Exactly."

"But," she says, emphasizing the word in a way that tells me I won't like what comes after, "you also said that we should call you out when we thought you were making a decision based on emotion instead of logic."

I cross my arms, too. "Spit it out, Everly."

"You have issues with this interview that are emotional, not logical. You know how important it is to come out of the gate strong with the release of *Nudge Out*. And you also know that our advertising budget alone isn't going to get us where we need to be so it's important to find out-of-the-box ways to meet our goals. It's what this business was built on. You couldn't have led us to where we are now without doing exactly that."

She leans forward like she wants to make sure I'm absorbing everything she says. "This business is healthy because we all believe in that vision. It's why *Business Success* named you one of their *Top Ten CEOs Under Thirty*, and it's why those investors are thinking of forking over so much cash. This interview with Bex Sterling exactly supports that vision."

I growl and look to the side. Deep down, I know that. It's what makes me so frustrated.

"So, talk to me. Help me understand why you are resisting this so much."

I don't want to admit to Everly that I'm worried about my peers thinking I sold out, or that I'm not a real business, or that I no longer take my company seriously if I do a frivolous interview on a YouTube channel. Would they make fun of me behind my back? To my face?

And I especially worry that I'll make a fool of myself in front of a big audience. I'm not a natural in front of the camera, so chances are pretty good that I'll end up being the punch line of jokes everywhere. And doing four interviews will give me quadruple the chance to royally embarrass myself. Since the content won't belong to my company, it's not like we'll have any say over something getting edited out.

And what about the fact that I'm attracted to Bex? She isn't the type of girl I normally date, and she definitely isn't the type to fit into my family. Bex is the kind of girl who thinks she should get everything she demands. I have experienced that enough in my life to know it isn't for me.

So obviously being attracted to her is a terrible idea, and I should stay as far away from her as possible.

Being attracted to her aside, what would my dad think about the interview? I run my hands down my face. If my dad found out I did an interview that was even more casual and less professional than my one in *Business Success*, he would definitely not be proud of me. I hate that I even care. But that's the only part that I'm willing to admit to Everly, so I say, "My dad will hate it."

"Your dad doesn't have to know."

Even if he doesn't ever find out, I shouldn't be spending the kind of time a multi-part interview would require when we have an app to launch. "This is clearly a time I should be focusing on the business, not doing four interviews for the same channel."

"This *is* focusing on your business. I can set up a meeting with Bex Sterling and be there to mediate so we can come to a mutual agreement on the terms."

There are so many things about this interview that I don't like. I can't agree to it.

"The bottom line is," Everly says, "you care about the health of this company. That's obvious in every single choice you've made. Make the healthy choice here, too."

If I put all my feelings about the interview aside, I know without a doubt that Everly is right. She's right about the interview, she's right that I would do anything for this company, and she's right that saying yes to Bex is a healthy choice for my company. But is it a healthy choice for *me*?

I'm sure it isn't, but against my better judgment, I find myself giving her a nod of permission to set up the meeting.

CHAPTER 5

Bex

I SPENT the morning with Nikki, going over the edited video for our Sterling Sisters segment, updating my schedule for the next two weeks, and brainstorming all of the ways we will advertise and interact with fans during the judging period for the Eddie Award. My roommates are all out working with clients, so once Nikki leaves, the place feels empty, which doesn't happen often. It's days like this, when I have hours of administrative tasks to do, that I like to take my laptop to a crowded coffee shop or deli to work.

But before I do that, I need to get Corbin Shields's publicist emailed since the interview with Roman isn't going to work out. I bring up the email draft Nikki has written and I'm tweaking the wording when I hear the front door open. A moment later, it opens a second time, and then I hear talking coming from the front of the inn. Curious, I get up from the desk by the big back windows of the gathering room and head to the lobby and then, following the voices, to the kitchen.

It's Addison and Ian—neither of whom I expected to be home right now—and they are mid-kiss when I walk in. Which I totally *would've* expected if I had known it was them.

"Check you two out, both home in the middle of the day."

"I only scheduled the first half of my day with clients," Addison says. "The rest of my day is here, organizing for a big job."

Ian opens the fridge and starts getting out items for sandwiches. "And since my afternoon is better with a boost of Addi, of course, I'm going to come home for lunch."

"Aww. You two are as sweet as ice cream on apple pie."

Addison joins Ian in the sandwich-making, standing shoulder to shoulder like they are magnets and can't help being stuck together when they're near. "What are you up to today?"

"About to send an email to Corbin Shields's publicist. Speaking of which, what is the deal with Roman? Other than last night and the wedding, I don't know him a ton, but he always seems guarded. Like he's trying to keep us from seeing the real him. Please tell me he wasn't like that in college, because if he was, I just can't see how you two became friends."

Ian shrugs as he piles enough meats and cheeses on a slice of bread that I am sure he'll never be able to get his mouth around it. "I don't know. Yeah, I guess I'd call it 'guarded.' It wasn't as bad in college, but he's always kind of been somewhat that way. Probably because his dad is about as intimidating as a starving mountain lion staring you down as he thinks about which part of you he's going to eat first."

I reach across the counter to grab an apple. All this food and talk of food is making me hungry. "And it makes Roman close himself off?"

Ian glances at me when he reaches for the mustard. "All I can say is that the University of Oregon was just far enough away from Lake Oswego that he could justify going home only once or twice a semester, and that we hated when he went home because he was a bit of a jerk when he came back. But I don't know. I guess I could sit down with him and have a heart-to-heart discussion where we try to really get to the root of his feelings so he can acknowledge where they are coming from."

I reach across the island counter and give Ian a playful smack on the arm. "You've leveled up your ability to deliver sarcasm. I am so proud." I take a big bite of my apple.

Ian takes a little bow, then puts the top slice of bread on his sandwich, admiring his handiwork. "All I can say is, regardless of anything else, he's a good guy. And a good friend."

Yeah. I sense that. And a part of me—the woman part—is drawn to that. And, okay, the jawline and those intriguing eyes fringed with the most amazing lashes. But the YouTuber part of me knows that if I put someone who is guarded in front of a camera, the audience won't connect with them no matter how easily they'd be able to connect with someone like Roman otherwise. It's good that he already told me no.

"And," Addison says as she puts the finishing touches on her sandwich, which, unlike Ian's, looks like a human could actually open their mouth wide enough to take a bite of, "you two look adorable together. You did at the wedding, too. I know you really just got on each other's nerves at the wedding, but I swear that there were sparks last night." She flashes me a wide smile. "You two should date!"

Luckily, I have already swallowed the bite of apple I'm chewing, or one of them would probably be wearing it. "Ha. No. No way. Any sparks that may or may not have been present are irrelevant because I don't date guys like that."

Ian's eyebrows draw together. "Guys like what?"

"You know," I say, waving my hand around like I'm trying to catch something so obvious I shouldn't need to define it. "The kind of guy who likes to be in charge, and is driven and opinionated."

"Oh," Ian says, an amused smile on his face, "so someone like you?"

"Exactly. There can only be one of us in a relationship. I grew up in a house with a mom and four sisters who all like to be in charge and are driven and opinionated. All five are happily married to guys who are easygoing, thoughtful, and willing to go along with any wild plan one of us comes up with."

Addison shakes her head. "That doesn't mean that's the only type of guy who will work out."

"Yes, it does." I punctuate it with a firm shake of my apple in Addison's direction. "Nikki married someone who also liked to be in charge, and was driven and opinionated, and their marriage was awful. I'm talking explosively awful.

Thankfully, they figured out how toxic they were for each other before they had kids.

"Then she met Dylan. He's kind, thoughtful, and easygoing, and they're adorable together. Being the youngest comes with drawbacks. Like getting hand-me-down underwear. *Underwear*, y'all! So you better believe I take the perks when I can get them. And one of them is having older siblings who make all the mistakes so I don't have to. I'm not about to make the same mistake Nikki did."

I study my apple, choosing the best next bite. "Besides, I can guarantee I will never see Roman Powell again. After last night, whenever you guys get together with him, I can tell you right now that he will move heaven and earth to make sure it only happens when I'm nowhere nearby."

The moment I bite down on my apple, my phone rings. I chew quickly as I pull it from my pocket and look at the screen. It isn't a number I have in my contacts, but it says it's from Gresham, Oregon. I finish chewing, then swallow and answer it.

"Hello, this is Bex Sterling."

"Hi, Bex. This is Everly Richins. I'm the marketing and social media manager at LivenUP."

I glance at Ian, my head tilted to the side. Isn't LivenUP Roman's company?

"I was wondering if you would be willing to come to Gresham for coffee this afternoon to meet with me and Roman Powell."

I did not see that coming at all. A big part of me has been glad that I might get to interview Corbin Shields instead. But beyond all the reasons why I want him over Roman Powell, what I want most is to honor my viewers' wishes. And they want Roman. It's enough to say yes to a second chance at working things out with him.

"Um, sure. I'd be happy to. Just text me the time and location."

After Everly says goodbye, I hang up the phone and stare at it for a good ten seconds as I try to make sense of what just happened. "Well, that was unexpected."

CHAPTER 6

Roman

I SET the tray holding three coffees and an assortment of creams and sugars down on the table. Then I sit in the spot I have claimed as "mine" since the first time I walked into this coffee shop the day I signed the papers on my current office building. Not that I actually drink my coffee here often, but I do come here daily.

Being in my own territory when meeting to discuss this mutually beneficial arrangement is better. Sure, I chose the location the last time I met with Bex, but it was clearly her place enough that she called it family. This is mine.

Everly sits in the seat next to me and grabs a cup of coffee from the tray. She removes the lid off and, while dumping in an obscene amount of sugar, says, "We need to do whatever it takes to make this happen."

I notice Bex through the window the moment she steps out of her car. She is dressed in dark jeans and a baby blue v-neck shirt that looks amazing on her if I am noticing that kind of thing. I kind of wish she would dress as inappropriately for the occasion as I had when we met at Buffalo Bill's Steakhouse. But this is a coffee shop. It's not like there's a wrong way to dress.

It doesn't matter. This is my place, and I am in charge of this meeting. I have the upper hand this time, and I am going to run the meeting my way from beginning to end.

The moment she steps through the doorway, I stand, ready to give my "I mean business" handshake. But her eyes don't immediately go to mine the way mine go to hers. She starts scanning the room, but before she gets to me, her eyes land on the manager, and both their faces light up in recognition.

"Roger!" Bex says, hurrying toward him as he comes around the counter.

"Bex Sterling," Roger says, giving her a hug in greeting. "It's been a while. How are you?"

As the two of them chat, I roll my shoulders back and flex my jaw, trying to keep from clenching it. I chose *my* place, and she is a long-lost BFF with the manager.

"Relax that drum solo," Everly says, pointedly looking at the two fingers I am tapping on the tabletop. "We want her to be comfortable because then she'll be more likely to give us what we want. Her knowing the manager is a good thing."

It doesn't stop my jaw from clenching again.

"Do you remember Marco?" Roger asks Bex. Then he turns his head toward the back of the store and shouts, "Hey, Marco. Come here a minute."

Then Marco comes out, and apparently she knows him,

too, and it's reunions all over again. I have never even seen Marco before. So Bex knows more people than I do at my own coffee shop?

Luckily, Bex's conversation with both men ends quickly, and her gaze shifts in my direction. She gives me a brilliant smile when she sees me, which I meet with my own hard smile as she walks to our table.

"Hello." She reaches out, shakes my hand and then Everly's, and then bangs her knee into the chair as she takes a seat. The sound is loud, and she hisses in a breath, wincing.

A smile tugs at my lips as I sit. It's not enough to make up for the fact that she has leveled out the playing field by knowing the people at my home field, but it definitely helps.

"Thank you so much for meeting with us," Everly says. "Roman and I have talked, and we decided that, even though the two of you have a difference of opinions on a few points, he would really like to do the interview. We are hoping that we can talk about a few of those differences so that we can come up with something mutually beneficial."

And this is why I hired and promoted Everly. She can take my "I hate everything Bex wants to do but still see the value in bringing in the new users" and turn it into something professional and courteous.

Bex sits straight in her chair, looking regal and professional, which is impressive, considering the critical look that is just beneath the surface. She is quiet for a moment, then says, "Interesting. Because when Roman and I talked last night, he didn't seem to think very highly of my channel."

Probably because it is a channel not meant to be thought of highly. It's just there for the sake of entertainment. I open my mouth to talk, but Everly must sense that what I am about to say won't get us the interview, so she touches my forearm to pause me.

"That was before he spent some time watching your videos. He especially liked your interview with Brooke McClellan."

By "watching your videos," Everly means that she forced me to watch five minutes of that interview.

"It's one of my personal favorites," Everly says. "I don't think I've ever laughed and sighed and cheered and cried so much in one fifteen-minute period. I've seen interviews with her before, but I never felt like I got to know her the way I did in your interview. That's actually what led me to your channel initially and got me to subscribe."

"Thank you," Bex says. "I'm so glad you connected with it."

I take a deep breath. I am being a jerk with my thoughts, and I need to stop. *This will help LivenUP*, I remind myself. And regardless of what I think of her channel, she is very good at what she does. "I would like to do the interview. But the reason I would like to is because we have a new app releasing, and I want to get the word out. That's my entire purpose."

"Roman," Bex says, and my chest lifts a little hearing my name on her lips, "I think we've had a bit of a miscommunication. I want you to get the word out. My plan all along was to help you with promoting your app. But that'll be most effective if people can connect with *you*. They aren't going to watch long enough to learn about your app if they don't."

"Fine."

"So you'll do the four-part interview and let me get personal?"

I look out across the coffee shop. This is a bad idea. I am used to running this company with my gut, and my gut is telling me to run far away from this woman and from this interview.

But, strangely, it is also telling me to stay. I don't know whether it's because of the investors, who want me to do something like this, or if it's because of Bex herself, but I can't deal with the conflicting messages. I just need to make a decision. So I give a curt nod.

Then something catches my eye—a mother and daughter who are standing in line, looking over at us as the daughter whispers to the mom. She looks like she is probably thirteen, and I do not want to relive the embarrassment of last night again when the two girls came over to our table. Not in front of one of my employees, and especially not a second time in front of Bex. Maybe they'll leave it at whispering about me from a distance.

But then the two of them break away from the line and walk over to our table. Instead of walking toward me, though, they head straight to Bex.

Bex greets them with the same big smile she gave Roger and Marco when she first walked in.

"Hi," the girl says. "You're Bex Sterling, right?"

"I am."

The girl's smile widens. "I'm a Bexlandian. I love your show! It's my favorite. I watch it, like, seriously, the second a new video comes out. And then my friends and I get together to rewatch it. My favorite episode is the one where you're bringing the happy birthday cake with the candles to your nephew, and their dog attacks your ankles, and the cake splats everywhere."

As the girl and Bex chat about how hilarious that was, what a mess it made, and how many times the girl watched it, I seriously question my choice. My target audience isn't kids who would be content watching fail videos all day long. It's adults who are looking to live their lives more fully. Adults with cash to spend on apps. And I definitely don't want myself lumped in with the birthday cake debacle.

I am turning to Everly to suggest we cut our losses while we can when the girl's mom speaks. "You're Roman Powell, right?" When I give a nod, she says, "I read your interview. I like that you admitted to wishing you could stay in bed some mornings and just laugh at funny memes, but that your responsibilities always get you out of bed early." The woman nods a few times. "I'm the same way."

I am never going to interview with *Business Success* again. And I definitely am not going to with Bex, either.

When the mother and daughter leave, I say, "Actually, the four-part personal interview isn't going to work out after all. Let's do just one, focusing only on the company and products."

Those hazel eyes of hers bore into mine. Like the golden ring around the edge of her iris has magical powers. Then, after a pause long enough that it makes me uncomfortable, she says, "Okay, I have an opening for that in a couple of months."

"Nothing sooner?" Everly asks. "Our new app releases in two weeks."

"Listen," Bex says, "between two weeks from now and six weeks from now, I am being judged for an Eddie Award. I have to put my best work forward during that time, and I'm not about to do the kind of interview that is going to get people to click away to a cat video thirty seconds in. Because that's what they will do if we have an interview like that."

"Roman," Everly says, her voice pleading.

But what am I supposed to do? Say yes to something I don't believe in? If a regular interview won't work with her audience, then my first instinct to walk away was right. It means her audience isn't mine. I am about to stand up and end the meeting, but Bex folds her arms and gives me a look that somehow keeps me in my seat.

"Did you not see what happened with that mother and daughter?" she asks.

"Yeah, I did. It was the same thing as what happened in the restaurant last night. Random strangers pulled out the insignificant facts instead of focusing on the important ones. That's not what I'm looking for."

"No. What you saw was someone who read an article about you and found a way to connect to you." She turns to see that the mother and daughter are just walking away from the counter after ordering. She calls out, "Kendall? Do you mind coming back for a second?"

I hadn't noticed that the two had given their names. When they come back to our table, Bex says, "Do you mind if I ask you a couple of questions?" The woman shakes her head, so Bex says, "You read the article about Roman, right? There were articles about nine other young CEOs. How many of those did you read?"

"All of them."

"I'm impressed that you remembered Roman's name. Do you remember the names of all of them?"

The woman lets out a breath that is equal parts laugh and snort. "Nope. None of them."

"Why do you think you remembered his?"

The woman blushes. "I don't know. I guess I just felt like I knew him more."

Bex nods. "Do you know what company Roman runs?"

"Yeah! LivenUP, right? You're the company that makes some great apps. I got the music one right in the middle of reading your article. I use it all the time."

Bex is smiling like the woman is telling her she thinks her puppy is cute. "And how many other company names do you remember?"

"I don't know. Two or three?"

Bex gives her a brilliant smile, then thanks her as she and her daughter go off to find a booth. Then Bex turns that brilliant smile on me. And she keeps it on me without saying a word.

Not that she needs to. I am a smart enough guy to get the point she is trying to make. Knowing that I wished I could shrug off responsibilities and laugh at memes got this woman to buy our app. This must be what the interviewers were calling the "spark" that they were looking for. Maybe sharing a tiny bit of me wouldn't hurt. As long as Bex keeps it to surface stuff.

"Fine. We'll let it get a little personal. Four parts."

The look of triumph on Bex's face is only there for a moment before it is replaced by a look of professionalism.

"Then you'll agree to a rapid-fire interview right now? This won't be released—it's just to help me decide on interview locations."

I can feel Everly's eyes on me, hoping I'll say yes. So I nod. I am used to doing hard things for work. How hard can this be?

Bex turns on her voice recorder, then leans forward on her elbows, meeting my eyes without flinching. "Okay, give me the first answer that comes to mind. Don't stop to think about it. Ready?" I nod, so she says, "First employee's name?"

"Daran."

"Where did you grow up?"

"Lake Oswego."

"Favorite thing to do outdoors as a kid?"

"Go camping for scouts."

"Favorite childhood memory?"

"Building a blanket fort in our family room with my brothers and eating ice cream in it."

"Favorite sport to watch?"

I pause, hopefully not long enough for her to notice. "Basketball."

"Favorite sport to play?"

"Racquetball."

"Favorite color?"

"Blue."

"Why did you pause when I asked what your favorite sport to watch was?"

Because the first thing that came to mind was dance competitions, and it would be one hundred degrees on the tip of Mount Hood before I admit that. "Trying to decide between basketball and hockey."

"Fair enough." She turns off the recorder and looks between me and Everly. "Okay, I'll contact you both by tomorrow at noon with a proposed schedule and filming location for our first interview." Then she grabs her cup of coffee for the first time, nods a goodbye, and walks out the door.

I am still staring after her while completely ignoring Everly's victorious grin as I wonder what, exactly, I just got myself into.

CHAPTER 7
Bex

I PULL into the parking lot at the Mirror Lake trailhead Saturday morning, and Enoch and I get out of the car. As Enoch gets all of the camera equipment ready, I bring up my notes on my phone and start going through them.

I'm glad that Roman was willing to meet so soon to film. I had other segments originally planned for the four-week judging period, and most of them were filmed and edited already. But when I became a finalist for the Eddie, I decided I wanted something more spectacular to post during the judging period. Which means I am so much further behind than I am comfortable with.

Tires sound on gravel, and I look up to see Roman pulling into the parking lot.

"Are you sure you're good to hike with that weight?" I ask my nephew.

"Of course!" he says, flexing his biceps. Not that the kid has an abundance of muscles, but what he has, he shows proudly. I should've known he'd be just fine. At least the hike isn't long or difficult.

"Remember to keep the camera rolling the whole time."

"I know, I know. 'We always find gems in the parts when the camera normally wouldn't have been rolling.'"

"And you even quote me. See? This is why you're the best cameraman." I put on my backpack which contains a few water bottles and a small first aid kit. When Roman gets out of his vehicle and nears, I call out, "Are you ready for this?"

Roman nods and smiles up at the trail. "It's been a long time since I've been up here."

Then he sizes up Enoch, and I am suddenly seeing my nephew through Roman's eyes. Young. Skinny. He has grown enough recently that he hasn't quite figured out how to use his new height. And his hair isn't so much the signature perfectly-styled-to-appear-messy look as it is an accidentally messy look.

"You're using a, what—fourteen-year-old—kid as a cameraman?"

Enoch doesn't see it as a rude comment. In fact, he puffs out his chest in pride that Roman thinks he's older than he is.

"He's twelve—"

"—and a half," Enoch cuts in.

"—and not only is he my nephew, but he's a kid who's interested in the filming side of the business and does a mighty fine job of it. So don't look at him like he's not legit."

Roman holds up his hands in surrender. "No offense meant at all. I think it's great to know what you want to do at such a young age." He looks at the trail again. "So, how does this work?"

He seems nervous. I am used to trying to make a guest feel comfortable during an interview, but sometimes people who aren't used to having a camera on them struggle with it a bit more. Hopefully, Roman will get used to it very quickly into our hike.

"Well, it starts with you being more like yourself." I see a flash of confusion cross his face for the briefest of moments before he is back to his guarded self, so I explain. "It's like your exterior isn't aligned with your interior. If you're not being authentic, viewers will pick up on it, even if they can't say exactly what the issue is."

"Got it, Barbara Walters."

I realize that it isn't nerves I'm witnessing—it's straight-up reluctance. Of course. The guy is way too confident and in charge for nerves. This is going to take some serious interviewing skills and a whole lot of patience. "We'll chat while we're hiking, then I'll ask a few questions at the lake while we stop and admire the beauty, and then we'll chat on the way back down. Sound good?"

We've barely made it far enough along the trail to not see the parking lot anymore when Roman stops and glances at the camera. I stop, too, hoping he isn't going to call it off because whether interviewing him during the judging period is the best idea or not, I have committed to it.

"I've got one request before we go too far," he says.

I cock an ear toward him. "Oh good. I was afraid it would be a demand."

The corners of his mouth lift in not quite a smile, but

something edging toward it. "Only because you're going to agree to it without it being a demand."

I raise an eyebrow, trying not to smile.

"You let me install Nudge Out on your phone, and you let it pick the location for our fourth interview."

I study him for a long moment like I am trying to decide if I should let him. Of course, I am going to say yes, because that sounds interesting and makes that fourth interview an unknown entity, which, coming from a guy who seems to like everything planned down to the last detail, makes it even more interesting. I kind of want to make him sweat a bit before I do.

Then I pull my phone from my back pocket, lift it to my face to unlock it, and hold it out toward him.

His fingers brush over my palm as he picks up my phone, and it sends a thrill straight to my heart. Again. This man is going to be the end of me. Why did I push for this interview?

I watch as the expression on his face changes from stoic to something resembling happiness as he installs the app on my phone and does whatever he is doing to make an app that isn't actually live yet work on my phone.

Then, he hands it back to me, and I look down at the blue and green Nudge Out icon that is now on my phone.

I always film an introduction to my guest separately and start the finished video with it, but I still need to lead into the interview, and I hadn't planned to do it like this. As we walk up the dirt trail, trees lining both sides of it and blocking out all sounds other than nature and the squeals of a couple of kids hiking with their family further up the trail, I fall into the rhythm of an interview.

"So you're the CEO of LivenUP, and your company has quite a few very successful apps, like Musicbound and Group Eat, but this one you just put on my phone is brand new. It releases today, even." It doesn't actually release today, but this video is going to air on the day it releases. "Tell us about it."

"People stay in their comfort zones because everything is nice and easy there." He glances up the trail as we walk, and then his eyes quickly come back to me. "There's a quote that says, 'Life begins at the end of your comfort zone.' People know that great things lie on the other side of whatever normal is for them, but most feel like it's such a huge, terrifying leap to try something new, or they don't know where to start.

"When you install this app on your phone and go about doing all the things you normally do, it'll learn what your comfort zone is. Then it'll nudge you to try something just outside of your comfort zone."

"I get it," I say as we walk, Enoch and the camera on us the whole time. "So the nudge it gives you is an easy thing since it's not too far out of what's normal for you. Nothing terrifying."

"Exactly. The more you do the things it nudges you to do, the more things you'll experience, the further you'll be stepping out of your comfort zone, and the more rich your life will become. There are great things out there for everyone, and you'll get to them if you take those little nudges."

"Wow. That sounds pretty amazing. So it's working right now on my phone?"

Roman nods. "In a week or so, after it gathers enough data, a notification will come up saying it's ready to suggest something new. When it does, you can tap the *Nudge Me Out* button, and we'll know where we'll be having our fourth interview."

My grin spreads wide, and I look right at the camera. "Usually, I try to have an interview in a location that has something to do with the person I'm interviewing—a place they know well, a place that feels at home to them, or one that has something to do with their job. Remember, Bexlandians, that Roman put the app on *my* phone, not his. Tell me in the comments if you're hoping that the fourth interview will be in a location I would've chosen for Roman, or if it'll be one that will nudge him—or shove him—right out of his own comfort zone."

Roman laughs, and the sound is magical. Partly because we are in some pretty dense woods where we can currently see no other humans and it mixes with the nature all around us. But mostly because it's something I hadn't expected from him at all.

"This entire interview series is well outside my comfort zone, so maybe if that fourth one is, too, I'll feel right at home."

This is good. He's relaxing. Letting his guard down a bit. He has a long way to go, but a teeny bit of authenticity is actually coming through.

"I'm guessing you've tested the Nudge Out app yourself. What's something the app has nudged you to try?"

"I play racquetball and lift weights. It suggested I try yoga."

"And did you?"

"Of course."

"What did you think?" I am suddenly picturing myself doing yoga next to him, the morning sun shining through the window on us, which is definitely not keeping my head in interview mode. I work to get it back.

"Six weeks later, I'm still doing it daily."

"Impressive." *Don't think about it, Bex. Stay in interview mode.* "Favorite pose?"

"Half pigeon."

"No."

"Why? What would you have guessed?"

I lift a shoulder. "One of the warrior poses, I guess."

We chat more about his company and Nudge Out as we hike the trail. It's steep in some sections, but there are handrails in places where it's especially steep. Most of the twenty-minute hike is easy, though. Easy enough that a lot of the trail, Enoch even walks backward in front of us so he can film our faces. Other times, he finds a rise or a boulder to climb onto so he can get a good location shot of us hiking.

The end of the trail opens onto the shore of Mirror Lake. The day is clear and absolutely stunning. The wind isn't blowing at all so the surface of the lake is still and is showing off exactly how it got its name. We soak in the sunshine as we walk around to the backside of the lake. From there, we can see almost the entirety of Mount Hood reflected in the waters along with the trees surrounding the lake, the blue skies, and the white puffy clouds.

We stand in silence for several long moments, enjoying the incredible display of nature around us while Enoch gets a lot of video so my viewers can experience it, too.

"I wish we had a canoe," Roman says.

I look at him in surprise. Really, I am impressed that he showed up in jeans, a t-shirt, and an athletic jacket on our hike instead of a suit. But when I picture Roman in a canoe, I have a hard time imagining him without the suit, and the mental image just looks wrong. "You like to canoe?"

"It's been a while. Since I was a kid."

"You were a Boy Scout, right?"

He nods. "This one time, we were camping by Estacada Lake, and a bunch of us were out in canoes. This kid named Justin was with me in mine, and a couple of scouts in another paddled over to us. We were all just horsing around and splashing each other, and then Justin leaped out of our canoe, nearly capsizing it."

"I got low to the base, holding onto the sides and steadying it, and Justin reached over the side and grabbed my oars. Then he swam with them to the other canoe, tossed them inside, and then climbed inside himself. As they paddled away, he laughed and told me good luck getting back in time for mess duty."

"What do you do?"

"I tried paddling with my arms which, of course, didn't work at all—I could barely touch the water. So, I stretched out in the base of the canoe, pulled my hat down low to keep the sun out of my eyes, and enjoyed the most peaceful nap of my life.

"Two hours later, the Scoutmaster showed up in a canoe,

gave mine a little shake to wake me up, and I was back on the shore not long after. When I got back into camp, dinner was ready, and Justin was looking not too happy that he had to take my place making it."

We both laugh. And suddenly the mental picture of him in a canoe on the lake isn't just him in it by himself, wearing a suit, but it's the two of us in it together. In shorts and t-shirts. We're both rowing, him putting those strong shoulder muscles to good use. And I look blissful.

Then I realize that I am probably staring at him with that blissful face—on camera!—so I quickly shake myself out of it. But I don't stop marveling at the look on his face. It's like the facade he's been hiding behind has dropped at least part-way, and I'm seeing him. The real him.

But then Enoch moves to the side for a different shot, his feet scuffling across the rocky dirt as he does, and it's as if the sound makes the facade shoot right back up into place. The guarded Roman is back.

As we head down the trail, Roman glances to where Enoch is walking beside us. "By the time we reach our cars, you'll probably have over an hour of footage. How long will the video be when it airs?"

"Twelve to fifteen minutes, depending on which angle we decide to take and what is going to keep the pacing moving along well."

"Then you'll be able to take out the story I told."

"Probably not."

"It's irrelevant."

"Nope."

"I want to approve the video before it goes up."

"You don't seem to have a lot of faith in what I do. Why did you say yes to the interview?"

He squints off into the woods. "I want our product to launch well."

"Okay, but why did you say yes to *me*? There are other ways to launch a product well."

"Off the record?"

I nod, but he looks at the camera. Enoch does a good job of trying to be unobtrusive and becoming invisible to most people I interview. But Roman can't seem to forget he's there. And, of course, Enoch knows to not stop the camera no matter what. I'll just edit out the stuff that shouldn't be there later.

Roman shakes his head. "I know better than to fall for that 'off the record' trick."

I don't hide my eye roll or my annoyed hand on my hip. Of course, he'd answer that way. This conversation is about how he doesn't trust me, after all.

"Let's turn the question to you instead. Why did you say yes to interviewing a guy who you knew wouldn't give you as good of a show as Corbin Shields would when you have an award on the line?"

I stop and look at him for a long time. I have to respect the fact that he will just come right out and say it like it is. "Because my fans are loyal to me, and I am loyal to them. They said they most wanted me to interview you, and since we have each other's backs, I'm interviewing you."

The tiniest bit of movement catches my eye from just off the path beside us, and I look to see a deer staring at us. I suck in a breath and mumble, barely moving my lips, "Don't make any sudden moves. A deer is watching us from your seven o'clock."

To his credit, Roman actually turns to look very slowly. The deer doesn't move. "Wow. Deer are usually afraid of people. It's unusual to see one this close without spooking it."

"I don't think she's afraid of us. I think that if it could kill us just with the power of an intense stare, we'd be goners."

"She doesn't want to kill us. Deer don't go after people."

"Are you sure? Like one hundred percent of the time they don't?" I don't dare move an inch for fear that if I move, the deer will, too.

"Ninety-nine percent of the time. My Scoutmaster told us that sometimes when people feed deer, they can become aggressive toward humans."

My heart rate rises even more. "They're aggressive because people give them food? That's the definition of biting the hand that feeds you," I hiss.

"I don't make up the rules." He puts a hand on my shoulder, nudging me in the direction of the path. "Let's just walk back, slowly."

All three of us take a few hesitant steps, Enoch still aiming the camera at the action. But I can't keep my eyes on the trail ahead because I can't stop staring off into the woods at the doe. The look the deer is giving us tells me that it definitely woke up and stepped in coyote dung first thing this morning. "I think people have been feeding this one." I can hear the quiver in my voice.

Roman turns to look, and the deer takes that as her cue to attack. She lowers her head and comes charging at us, which is something I thought that only male deer did, but apparently, I was wrong.

The three of us take off running in the opposite direction of her—through the trees and brush and weeds and dirt and rocks. Roman grabs my hand, and we jump over a fallen tree trunk. Enoch races past us, his long legs and thin body propelling him over obstacles with no problem even while carrying the camera. He manages to get quite a distance in front of us quickly, and then he stops so he can aim the camera at the action.

After seeing him run on this uneven terrain, I know I don't need to worry about him. I need to worry about the angry deer that is still running after us like we're the embodiment of everything wrong in Deer World and chasing us away is the only path to justice.

Then the deer makes a sound that is somewhere between a bark and a gigantic prehistoric bird squawk, and I pick up the pace. The doe is definitely looking to murder us. She doesn't have antlers, so maybe she plans to kick us or stomp on us or… I have no idea how deer typically take down humans they are inexplicably angry at. Are deer like cheetahs and can only run for a short amount of time? Or can they run indefinitely?

I look over my shoulder and see she is way too close. I scream as my feet hit a stream that runs through the undergrowth, making me slip and fall flat on my back in the water. It takes me a moment before I'm able to take another breath after the one I had was forced out of me, even though I'm panicked and feel the need to get up quickly so I can keep trying to escape. When I open my eyes, all I can see is

Roman, smiling an actual smile and holding out a hand to me.

"Where's the deer? Is it about to attack?"

He shakes his head. "That scream of yours scared it off. We probably should've just started with that instead of running."

As he pulls me to my feet, I take several heaving breaths, trying to get my lungs to catch up after all the running and the terror and the fall. Then I look at Enoch, who has the camera aimed at me. "Please tell me you got that."

"Every last bit," my nephew says, grinning. "The running, the chasing, the angry deer sounds, the epic fall—all of it."

At least there's that. I try brushing myself off, but there isn't much I can do about how wet I am. The day has been decently warm, but we are in the shade now and my clothes are soaked. I wrap my arms around myself and have to work to keep my teeth from chattering.

"Here," Roman says, taking off his jacket and sliding it around my shoulders. He keeps his hands on my shoulders a moment, like he maybe wants to pull me close to warm me up, but then thinks better of it quickly. He drops his hands, but I can still feel the heat of where they've been, warming me far more than they should've been able to.

His jacket holds his scent, though. One I didn't even realize he had until now, as I am wrapped in it. It's nice—it's as warm and comforting as his jacket, yet it smells clean, too. Like maybe it's from his body wash, and it holds the scent of someone who knows what they want and isn't afraid to go after it.

He looks off in the direction of the path we're supposed to be on, and I take the moment to admire the way the part of his jaw by his ear curves down to his jawline, highlighting the dark stubble. And the way his dark hair teeters on the edge of being just short enough and styled enough to show he is a respectable businessman and long enough and just barely disheveled enough to show that there is more to him than that. It's too bad he has the same need to be in charge that I do because he is one very attractive man.

He's looking at me in a way I can't quite interpret. Enoch has the camera mostly on me right now, getting more of the backside of Roman. I wish he had it aimed right at Roman's face so I could watch it back as many times as needed to figure it out. "Um," my eyes dart to the direction we'd just come from, "do you think the deer will be waiting for us?"

He smiles at me in a way that tells me it's just for me. He's not thinking about the camera at all. It is one of the most beautiful things I've ever seen, and I'm suddenly very aware that the camera is on me and I'm staring at him with that blissful face again.

"I think you scared it enough that if it sees us, it'll run in the opposite direction now."

I don't realize how far we have traveled away from the path until we spend what feels like an hour to get back to it and then down the path to the parking lot. As I near my car and Enoch heads to the back passenger's door to lay down the camera equipment, Roman stops me.

"You asked why I was willing to do the interview with you."

My eyebrows shoot up. I didn't think I'd ever get an answer from him.

"It's because of your sense of loyalty and because you're willing to stand your ground." His mouth quirks up in a smile. "Except in the case of trying to run over a stream while being chased by a sweet deer, of course."

"I may not have stood my ground, but let's remember that I did manage to scare off the beast."

Roman seems amused that I call it a "beast." But it definitely isn't a "sweet deer." Maybe he's forgetting the sounds it made. Or the way it looked at us like it needed to avenge the deaths of every deer that ever lived.

"And it was a pretty impressive scare-off if I do say so myself. If it was impressive enough to also scare you off from another interview…"

"Nah. I didn't get to where I am by being easily scared off."

I may not have been thrilled about interviewing Roman when I first agreed to it, but it surprises me how much I want us to continue now. "Are you free during the first half of the week? The episodes will only air once a week, but I don't want to be so tight on editing, and the more time I get to promote, the better it will be for both of us."

He gives me a smile that is so adorable it makes my insides flutter. Then he says, "I'll check out my schedule and get back to you on that."

I know he is very much the wrong guy for me. But that doesn't stop me from noticing how right he looks as he walks back to his car.

CHAPTER 8

Roman

"Roman!" my mom says as she puts her hands on the tops of my arms and kisses both of my cheeks. "I'm so glad you could make it!"

I like that my mom is always so happy to see me. And that she acts like it's my choice to come for Sunday dinners, even when we all know it's mandatory if you're the offspring of Evelyn and Richmond Powell.

"Come in, come in! Your brothers are already here." She puts her arm in mine and walks me to the drawing room that's just off the dining room. Most families have a living room—or they would even call this space a family room—but not the Powells. We have a drawing room like it's the eighteenth century and we're nobility.

My two brothers are already in the room, standing, with drinks in their hands. The brother just younger than me, Drake, is next to his wife, Claire. They're a good match. Claire has the classy look and ability to host an event that's silently required of Powell wives. But she's also smart and has big ambitions.

Not Briza, though. She's the woman my youngest brother, Legend, has brought to the previous two dinners. She's strictly shallow eye candy, like most women my brother dates. Which would be fine, except Legend seems to need someone who is less predictable. I don't think I'll see her at too many more family dinners.

It takes me aback when I realize that Briza is exactly like most of the women I've dated, too. *Huh.* Maybe that's why my relationships never last long.

My brothers turn to look at me as I walk in, all big smiles.

"Hey, bro." Drake claps me on the shoulder. "Why so serious?" He glances at my feet. "Don't tell me you wore serious socks today."

"Ha ha."

"Don't listen to him," Claire says. "I read the article, and I thought it was great."

Legend nods. "Top notch. I especially liked the part about how your favorite scent is the smell of chocolate chip cookies baking. I wish I could've been there to see the look on your face when the interviewer asked you if that's the scent a woman who was interested in you should wear."

I'm about to make a show of acting like I'm going to leave because of their comments, but when I turn, my dad is just walking into the room from his office. "Now don't give your brother a hard time. He's learned from his mistakes and won't be so forthcoming on personal details next time. You just wait until you have your first interview with a magazine journalist—you'll find out how wily they are."

"And when you do," Drake says, "follow my lead, not Roman's."

Surprisingly, I actually enjoyed the interview with Bex yesterday, and I've spent the rest of the day—and today—thinking about her.

But all day today, I've been second-guessing the wisdom of doing the interview in the first place. As if it isn't bad enough that my brothers are razzing me about sharing personal stuff in my *Business Success* interview—just like I shared personal things with Bex in her interview, which I will never tell any of them about—my dad has to come in and defend me, like I'm too weak to stand on my own two feet. The icing on the cake is Drake reminding everyone that his first interview made our dad proud enough that it earned him a trip down the Columbia.

Of course, I could pay for myself to take a trip down the Columbia at any time. It isn't about the money, though, or the actual trip itself. It isn't about camping or rafting or water or even spending time together. It's about my dad deeming something I do as worthy enough to warrant the trip.

And I'm not going to make my dad proud enough to earn my own trip unless I get the investors on board, which isn't going to happen if I don't do the interviews with Bex. It's a catch-22 that makes me want to leave this dinner for real.

Drake's reminder must've made my dad think about the trip as well, because he says, "Speaking of which, how are things going with the investors?"

"Good. They have some requests we're working on

meeting right now. But they seem ready to get on board." I shoot my mom a glance, hoping dinner is ready so the subject can change before my dad asks more questions.

"Briza," my mom says, turning to her, "Legend mentioned that you just finished midterms for your final semester. How did that go?"

I take a relieved breath as Briza talks excitedly about a public relations class that had a simulated public image issue to resolve for a fictitious client. Both of my parents beam, probably because she's shaping up to be a perfect potential Powell daughter-in-law. A docile trophy wife who can plan parties and look pretty.

But neither Drake's wife nor my mom is docile or shallow eye candy. I haven't realized it before, but maybe all Powell men need someone strong and driven at their side. Maybe that's what I need. But for now, I'm just glad my dad isn't asking me any more questions.

Until my parents' personal chef steps into the room and says that dinner is ready to be served. As we walk toward the dining table that separates the drawing room from the open kitchen, my dad says, "It's been a while since you've brought a woman to a family dinner."

"I'm not dating anyone right now." The bigger truth is, it's been a while since I've wanted to subject anyone to our family dinners. I imagine Bex coming to dinner and talking about her YouTube channel and how she likes to get personal with guests. Then I imagine how my dad would react and how much he would despise her work and probably everything about her. And how Bex would stand strong and not let something like the intimidating presence of Dr.

Richmond Powell IV, D.B.A. make her back down from her convictions.

Actually, I really like the thought of that showdown. It would definitely make Sunday dinners more interesting.

I feel a notification on my phone, so I sneak a peek. It's an email from Tarak, the guy from *Business Success* who interviewed me. He's asking me—and not for the first time—to join him on a panel about social media at the *PNW Open for Business* convention. I'm going to ignore it, just like I have the others.

At every weekly dinner, everyone gives an update on what's going on at their jobs. Drake talks about his work as a business strategist who just helped another Fortune 500 company. I update about my business, too, but keep it to how our release plans are going for Nudge Out. Legend talks about a new playground he just designed. Playground equipment isn't the direction our dad envisioned Legend using his architecture degree, but it fits him. And since he's the youngest and can do no wrong, going in an unexpected direction is exactly what earned him his trip down the Columbia.

As everyone talks, all I can think about is texting Bex. It takes me by surprise that my method of getting myself out of a family dinner is wanting to talk to the woman whose interviews have caused me so much stress. But I actually enjoyed getting to see her in action and getting to know her better. I smile just thinking about that deer chasing us and the look on her face when I offered a hand to pull her up after she slipped into the creek. Or especially when I took off my jacket and wrapped it around her.

Like every Sunday dinner right about the time the main course is served, my dad tells a story or two about something that happened in some business meeting or business get-together of his. This one is about a social gathering one of his executives hosted at their house. It sounds like they had a dozen or so guests and that the guy's adult son, Bennett, was there as well.

"Everyone was in small groups, sipping their drinks and eating refreshments, when, suddenly, the woman Bennett brought to the reception slaps him right across the face and then storms out of the place. Of course, Bennett just stands there, stunned and looking sheepish, while things get uncomfortable for everyone in the room. We didn't hear what Bennett said to cause her to react, but there were whispers that he made a joke about a gift she sent to his office after he lost a big client."

My mom shakes her head. "Why he thought that bringing up something personal between the two of them at a get-together with business associates was a good idea—and to make a joke about it, nonetheless—is beyond me."

"Bennett's parents were so ashamed," my dad continues. "I had to take Roy aside and assure him that no one looked down on him just because his kid made a poor choice that suddenly became everyone's business. But we all knew that everyone was, indeed, looking down on them."

Before I have a chance to think about what I'm doing, I find myself standing up, my phone in my hand. "If you'll please excuse me, this is a business call I have to take."

I walk back into the drawing room and keep going out the doors to the patio. I don't know why I'm out here—I haven't gotten a phone call. All I know is that I have to get out of the dining room with all the judgment, and the only acceptable reason for leaving is to take a business call. That, and I've been thinking of Bex, and hearing my dad's story makes me want to see her. To call her. To set up a time for our next interview.

Which is foolhardy and irrational. Hearing my dad all evening should've put me in a mind to call off the rest of the interviews and talk her into not airing the first one. As I think about all the things I shared with her—not just on audio or on paper, either, but on video where there will be no mistaking what I said—I know they're things that will disappoint my dad greatly.

Hah. That's an understatement. His reaction would probably be more along the lines of writing me out of his will. I can imagine the will reading right now: *And because Roman went on video with a site inelegant enough to be named "Bexlandia" and shared that he liked the Half Pigeon Pose and once got trapped on a lake in a canoe without paddles, I bequeath to him exactly one item—something I bought especially with him in mind: An outhouse by a rundown cabin in the Mount Hood National Forest.*

But instead of reacting like a sane human would in this situation, I call Bex. I'm playing with fire, and I know it. But for some inexplicable reason, those flames are drawing me to their warmth.

The phone rings twice before I hear her voice. "You've reached the voicemail of Bex Sterling. If you are calling with complaints about the previous interview or to make any more requests on what should be cut and what is allowed to be aired, please hang up and don't try again. If you are calling to schedule the next interview, please remain on the line."

I chuckle. Hearing her voice is definitely what I need to make it through the rest of this Sunday dinner.

"Oh, wow. That was close to an actual laugh. Does this mean you're calling to set up the next interview?"

"I told you I would, and I'm a man of my word."

"Spoken like a true Boy Scout."

"I'm free Wednesday and Thursday in the evenings. What do you have in mind for a location?"

"That depends. Tell me about racquetball."

"Okay. It's a sport played with a racquet and a hollow rubber ball, with two or four people, usually in an indoor court." With as into personal details as Bex is, I know that's not what she's asking for, but I can't help myself. I feel like a rebel today.

"Fascinating," Bex says, her voice monotone. "I can see why you chose it as your sport."

"The description was what sold me, too."

"It's not the sport most kids pick. Tell me why you really chose it."

"I didn't—my dad chose it for me."

"Interesting. Do you always do what your dad tells you to?"

"If I did, I'd be working at his company instead of owning my own."

"Fair enough. So tell me, what sport would you have chosen?"

"You're not recording this, are you?"

"Roman." I can practically hear her eyes rolling in that one word.

I glance toward the dining room windows where my family sits, eating dinner without me. "I played all the usual sports when I was young, and I was terrible at all of them."

This time, Bex chuckles. The sound is breathy and beautiful. "Big, strong, athletic you? I have a hard time picturing that."

"I wouldn't have called myself any of those things back then. In third grade, my mom decided that I would do better at sports if I had better awareness of my body and better coordination, so she enrolled me in dance classes. I still don't know how she talked my dad into it. I was embarrassed at first, especially because I was just as bad at it as I was at soccer, baseball, basketball, and football. But I got good at it and really liked it."

"Wow. I did not see that answer coming. Did you dance competitively?"

"Yeah."

"How long did you dance for?"

"Just until sixth grade. Then, one of my friends said something that really hurt my feelings, and I cried to my mom about it. My dad came in, said that I shouldn't have gotten my feelings hurt over something like that, and blamed my 'emotional state' on dance. He said it was time for a more manly sport, and since racquetball was his sport, that's what they signed me up for."

I can't believe I'm telling her all this. I haven't told a soul about it, ever. I rub at the tingling on the back of my neck, then pull at my shirt collar. Assuming she's going to push for more information, I start thinking of a response to shut her down. To my surprise, she backs off and goes a different direction, and I'm grateful.

"You listed it as your favorite sport, though, so I'm guessing you fell in love with it on your own at some point."

"My mom had been right about dance. By the time I started racquetball, I was significantly more athletic, and I got good at it quickly. It's easy to love a sport you can win at."

"That I have no problem picturing."

I smile just thinking of her picturing me playing racquetball. I hope she likes what she sees.

"Okay, how about we meet for the next interview on Wednesday at seven p.m.?"

"Seven it is."

"I'll text you the address by Wednesday afternoon. No showing up in a suit and tie. I suggest something more along the lines of athletic shorts, shirt, and shoes." She's silent for a long moment, then she says, "I'm glad that at the beginning of the phone call, you didn't hang up and not try again."

"Me, too."

But as I hang up and walk back into my parents' house to rejoin Sunday dinner, I wonder what in the world I've been thinking. Had it been anyone other than Bex, I actually would've hung up and not tried again. No, actually, I never would've called in the first place.

When it comes to Bex Sterling, I'm definitely playing with fire.

CHAPTER 9

Bex

ANYTIME I FILM a segment for my channel, I send all the footage to my sister, Nikki, along with a list of things I want to make sure make it into the final cut. Then Nikki does her magic, sends a draft of the video to me, and we go through it together, either in person or over FaceTime, and talk about edits.

Today, I've been working with Nikki over video chat, and I've spent the past forty-five minutes watching Roman as we go through the footage. I pause it at the spot when we're next to the lake and he's talking about canoeing, and switch the phone camera so that Nikki can see my screen. "I swear you can see the moment right *here* when he lets his guard down. Did you notice it when you were editing?"

"I did. I didn't know your lock-picking skills had reached a level capable of unlocking defenses as secure as this guy's. I'm impressed."

"I don't know. He noticed they were down like two seconds later and put them right back into place."

"But you got them down a second time, so there's hope."

They actually came down a third time when we were talking on the phone yesterday. During our first dinner at Buffalo Bill's Steakhouse, I never would've guessed that he'd let his guard down enough to tell me that story about dance and racquetball. I would've listened to his stories about both for an hour, but I know those defenses are poised and ready to snap right back into place at the slightest misstep, so I backed away slowly. Someday, I vow, I'll get them down for more than just a small moment.

Nikki and I get to the part of the video that shows the walk back, where I had all my focus on the murderous deer and hadn't been able to give any attention to Roman. But I'm paying close attention to him now.

I see the moment that shock and worry cross his face at seeing the deer's hollow stare, but unlike mine, Roman's expression quickly turns to confidence. I see his face when we're running and he reaches for my hand. And then the look of amusement and concern as he reaches out to help me up after I scream and fall flat on my back in the stream.

I pause the video on that expression of his, mentally thanking Enoch for his camera skills and for keeping it running the whole time, even with all the chaos going on. I'm going to have to thank the kid with copious amounts of Taco Bell, Red Vines, and Mountain Dew—his three favorite things that he doesn't get often.

I realize I've been staring—possibly a little dreamily—at the video when I see from the corner of my eye Nikki shaking her head. I'd forgotten that my sister could see me, and I really hope I haven't actually reached out and touched Roman's face on the screen like I wanted to. "What? He's cute."

Nikki nods. "He really is. Before I saw this interview, all I got from you was how much he irritated you, so I didn't think you'd noticed. But girl, between what I saw while editing and what I'm seeing now, you have definitely noticed."

"It was obvious in the footage?"

"Oh, no—I'm sure it wasn't obvious at all. To blind people."

Heat rises to my cheeks, and for a second, I feel the familiar resistance that makes me want to edit it out. I learned long ago how to push past my fear of being vulnerable on camera, though. Letting my audience see the real me is how they connect with me.

"Do you know what? It's fine. I'm betting a big reason as to why they voted him as the person they most wanted me to interview was because they saw how good-looking he was and wanted to get to know him more. They'll be feeling it, too, so it's okay if they see it from me."

"Which is why I kept so much of it in there."

"There was more that you cut?" Because I've seen plenty of myself very much noticing Roman's attractiveness.

"Enough for a lengthy compilation video. Want me to put together one? I'm betting I can find a great soundtrack to go with it."

"That's a hard no. It's fine if my fans really commiserate because they're feeling the same things. It's not fine if they start making up a relationship name for us. Roman isn't the kind of guy I can fall for."

"If you say so."

"All right, Nikki. You can stop giving me the 'It's so cute you don't see the things that I, as the older sister, can see.' It doesn't matter how very attractive Roman is—he's the wrong type of guy for me, and I will not be falling for him."

Nikki makes a show of wiping the amused expression off her face and replacing it with a neutral one. As we get back to work, I make sure I don't stare dreamily at the screen even once.

I can do that later when Nikki isn't watching.

I manage to stop thinking about Roman once we finalize the video for our first interview. Then I actually get work done on some ads, plan some future videos, reply to comments, write a few newsletters, and respond to an interview request. I haven't even realized how much time has passed until Peyton gets home. As soon as she comes into the inn, she walks into the gathering room and plops down on one of the couches. I save what I'm working on, close my laptop, and go to the end of the room where Peyton is.

"You're not your normal, peppy self. What's up?"

Peyton takes in a deep breath as she lifts her hands in an exaggerated shrug, then lets her arms fall to the couch as she exhales. "Between my biggest client telling me they 'no longer needed my services' on Friday, my crappy date on Saturday, and Max still being gone on a photography trip to the Cascades, I just can't seem to get out of my funk. You should have seen the butternut rolls I made at a client's home today. Even they were sad. Tell me I have good things going on in my life."

"Well, first of all," I say, "you have awesome clients who love you. More than you can handle. Your biggest client didn't treat you as well as the others, and now you'll be able to spend more time with the ones who do."

"True…"

"As far as dating, you are one step closer to finding the right guy, so cross that off your list." That one doesn't make Peyton perk up as much as the first, so I keep going. "I've had your butternut rolls, and I would eat a dozen regardless of how sad-looking they were. And just because one of your best friends is beyond cell reception in the Cascades doesn't mean you don't have a houseful of best friends here."

"Thanks, Bex."

"Do you know what you need? A dance party." I pull out my phone and start looking through my playlists for the perfect one.

"Bex, I'm too tired for a dance party."

"That's because there's no music playing right now. Just wait. You'll see." As I stand up, I notice Addison's car pull into the drive. Perfect. I walk to the stairs at the base of the lobby and call up, "Timini! Mandatory dance party in the gathering room!"

Within seconds, the stairs pound as Timini runs down them. "Dance party? I've needed that all day." Timini reaches the bottom of the stairs just as Addison opens the front door, so Timini loops her arm in Addison's and leads her to the gathering room, too.

As I pair my phone with the speakers, I say, "Peyton's

feeling down. You two pull her off that couch and we'll all pull her out of her funk." I start playing the music loud enough that Ian's grandma, Shirley, and her friend and now roomie, Carol, could probably have their own dance party at their house next door.

Then I set my phone to start recording video and place it on the mantel. And then we all start dancing. My roommates are used to me videoing random things and trust that I'll get approval from them before ever posting anything online. Now they expect me to film things like this.

Not only are these types of situations often perfect—you never know when a three-second clip of a dance party will liven up a video or provide the perfect humor—but my roommates enjoy having this time of our lives documented. Maybe we'll get together when we're all in our eighties for roommate reunions and watch these videos of us having fun and just being there for each other.

At first, Peyton only dances half-heartedly, no matter how much energy Addison, Timini, and I put into it. It only takes a couple of songs, though, before we're all singing along to the chorus of Rachel Platten's *Fight Song* and jumping up and down like we're kids at our first middle school dance.

We're still going strong when the front door opens a couple of minutes later and a confused Ian walks into the lobby. The confusion changes to happiness soon after, and he immediately comes into the room and starts dancing alongside Addison. I love that he so easily joins in whatever wacky thing we're doing. I wish Roman was here right now to join in, too.

Whoa. I've had exactly one interview and one phone call with him that have gone decently, and suddenly I'm wishing he'd show up to a roommate dance party? Clearly, I watched too much of him on that video today. I need to find a way to stop thinking about him so often. Just as soon as I get our next interview planned.

And then have the interview.

And then plan and carry out the next two.

And edit those three.

And release them and promote them all.

Okay, new plan: I just need to not allow myself to think of him anytime I'm not doing one of those things. Because he's the wrong guy, and I'm not about to fall for him.

As the song quiets near the end, a grinning, breathing-heavy Peyton says, "Holy guacamole, this is fun. Can we make mandatory dance parties an official thing?"

I walk right out to the lobby where we keep the roommate calendar and message board and pull out a pad of sticky notes. In as big of letters as will fit, I write *Mandatory dance party every Monday night* and stick it to the board.

There. It's official.

And while I'm writing it and sticking it up, I congratulate myself on going a full twelve seconds without thinking of Roman. This is going to be no problem at all.

CHAPTER 10
Roman

I PULL into the parking lot of the address Bex texted me, fully expecting to see a recreation center or some other building that might house a racquetball court since that was the direction she had taken our phone call. Instead, there are outdoor courts similar to tennis courts, but a bit smaller. I might've thought I was in the wrong place, but Bex is on the court with one of her roommates, a guy I recognize from Ian's wedding, and her videographer nephew, Enoch.

I like sports fine. I like them a lot, actually. What I don't like is walking onto the courts for a video interview while wearing gym clothes instead of a business suit. As I step through the gates onto their court, I'm even more wary as I notice they are holding paddles instead of racquets.

From the look on Bex's face as she takes me in, she is at least appreciating my clothing choice. Maybe it's a good thing I went for the shirt that shows off my chest and shoulder muscles. And she is looking pretty amazing in her tennis skirt and tank top.

"Hey, Roman. You remember Peyton and Max?"

I say hi and shake both of their hands. I'm glad Bex reminded me of their names because I hadn't remembered them at all. Then I say hi and shake Enoch's hand before I turn to Bex. "Couldn't get a reservation at a racquetball court?"

"Didn't even try."

I eye her. "So instead, we are going to play pickleball."

I must've made a face because her responding grin shows all of her teeth and is mischievous. And beautiful. "Yep. For two reasons. First: I didn't want to play against you in a sport you dominate at. Plus, racquetball is noisy and not conducive at all to interviewing. And second: you explaining your Nudge Out app inspired me to choose something similar to what you liked but a departure from your normal. A nudge out of your comfort zone."

So we are going to have the interview *while playing pickleball*. A sport I've never played before. One that I have never even watched before. I have a vague sense of it being something like life-sized ping pong. This is a far cry from the "across a desk from each other" interview I requested. Knowledge of this is definitely going into a vault to be kept far from my dad and brothers. And everyone else I know.

And I am never letting Everly put me in the company's social media plan again.

Luckily, Bex tells me about the rules and how the game is played and even lets me warm up a bit and try serving a few times before the camera starts rolling. Which is good, because those balls are so light that I assume it takes a lot more force to get them to where they need to go than they actually need. In fact, I really have to hold back.

I pick up the ball that has holes in it, like a whiffle ball from games when I was little, and walk to the back of the court. "Can we realistically carry on an interview while playing?"

"Yep. I find it helps calm the nerves a bit since all of the focus isn't on the interview and all its trappings. I'm hoping that it'll help you drop your guard a bit."

It definitely isn't doing that. I regret feeling so bold on Sunday when I talked about playing racquetball and am seriously rethinking the wisdom of saying yes to these interviews in general.

She walks over to me and presses down on my shoulders with her wrists, since her hand is holding a paddle, and my heart rate ramps up just having her so close. "Relax these muscles. You're wearing your seriousness like a suit of armor, and it's hiding what you've really got inside. People will connect with what you're saying about your products more if they can connect with you."

I roll my shoulders and shake out my arms. My dad and brothers are never going to see this. It's fine. All those men and women I hang out with at business receptions? They aren't going to see this, either. None of them spend their time watching YouTubers. This is purely for a demographic of people who are our target audience for our products. I'm speaking to them.

"You ready?"

I nod, so she nods to Enoch, and he starts filming.

"Hello, Bexlandians! We are back for our second interview with Roman Powell, the CEO of LivenUP. He has been playing racquetball for the past, what? Sixteen years? In the spirit of their new app that just released, Nudge Out, I decided we'd nudge Roman out of his comfort zone and try a completely new-to-him sport—pickleball!"

"Now, if you haven't heard of *Nudge Out* yet, I've got a link to our first interview below." She holds up her phone. "*Nudge Out* is an app that Roman put on my phone at the beginning of our previous interview. I put in the information it asked for, and it's just been sitting there, doing its thing, gathering data so it can suggest the best ways to nudge *me* out of *my* personal comfort zone. If you're curious about what that is, stay tuned for our fourth interview, because we are going to let the app decide where that will be."

Good. I'm glad she's talking up the app so much.

"We are going to start with Roman serving." She hands me the ball, and her fingers brush mine. It's like an electrical charge zips right up my arm just from the feel of her hand on mine, and it lights me up enough that I am suddenly more than ready to play. I serve the ball to Peyton, who is across the court from Bex. I have played enough sports to be able to hit a ball with a paddle just fine, but I am having trouble always using the right amount of force when I'm accustomed to playing a sport that requires so much more.

Luckily, Bex doesn't start off with interview questions so I can concentrate on not looking like a fool. Especially because simply being around Bex is occupying more and more of my attention, leaving less for paying attention to what I'm supposed to actually have my focus on.

I do pretty well for the first eight or ten times I hit the ball, but then I have to lunge for a ball, backhanding it as I do, and it doesn't even land in the court—it hits straight into the chain-link fence surrounding the court.

Bex laughs. "I can always tell when you revert to your racquetball roots because the sound of you hitting the ball is the same as that."

With as different as the racquets, the ball, and the court are, it surprises me that I catch that familiar sound, too. It makes me crave a game of racquetball, and suddenly, I'm picturing it with just Bex and me on the court. Getting in a good workout, competing, sweating together, and bumping up against each other. Then maybe leaning against the wall facing each other as we catch our breaths. And then kissing. A good amount of kissing.

The thought distracts me so much that when I pick up the ball I missed, I can't even remember whether it's my team's ball or Peyton's and Max's, let alone which one of them is supposed to serve it next. Thankfully, Max stands just behind the back line, looking like he's ready to serve, his eyes on me, so I toss it to him.

I've got to keep my head in the game, especially with that camera running. Besides, it doesn't matter how attracted I am to Bex—it only seems like it could work when I'm here with her in *Bexlandia World.* The real world is much more complicated, and just the thought of the two of us together in it and how much that would upend my world is all it takes to get me paying attention to that ball I just hit back to the other side.

"So..." Bex says, then pauses as Max calls out the score—

seven, six, one—and then serves the ball, "*Nudge Out* isn't your company's first app." She hits the ball back. "You have some pretty remarkable ones. Which one would you suggest for the four of us?"

"*Group Eat*. It's kind of like Pandora, except instead of picking your music, it picks a restaurant, and instead of for one person, it can do it for a group." I hit the ball back. Maybe I *can* interview and play at the same time. It's definitely easier than thinking of Bex while trying to play.

"You can set it to automatically detect when you're at a restaurant by using location services, you can log whenever you go to a restaurant, or you can just put in your favorite restaurants."

Bex misses the ball, so she picks it up and uses her paddle to send it over the net to Max.

"Each time you go out, just log if anyone else is with you —your significant other, friends, family, co-workers—and rate how much each person liked the restaurant out of five stars. If anyone that you go with has the app on their phone, you can just add them as a friend, and they can log all their own information."

I hit the ball back, and it goes right to the back corner of Max's side, and he misses the ball. Nice. Even during an interview. So the serve goes to Peyton.

"Eight, six, two," Peyton calls out and then serves the ball.

"Let's say we're going out to dinner." I hit the ball back to their side of the court. "We could go into the app, tell it that the four of us are going, and tap *Where should we eat?* It'll look at where we've eaten and liked in the past, find commonalities in the types of food offered in our favorite restaurants, and suggest a restaurant that all four of us will like."

Bex hits the ball to Peyton, who hits it quickly back.

"So," I say as I return the ball, "it solves the all-too-common issue of one person asking 'Where do you want to eat?' and the other one saying, 'I don't know. Where do you want to eat?'" I motion to Peyton and Max. "You should get the app, and see how much more smoothly your next date together goes."

"Oh," both Max and Peyton stumble out. "No—" And then they motion back and forth to each other, making Max barely able to hit the ball back over the net toward me. Then Peyton manages to blurt, "We're just friends."

Wow, did I read that wrong. It throws me off just enough that I nearly miss the ball that has come clearly to me. I have to rush, lunge, and backhand the ball with all of my might to get it. It registers somewhere in the recesses of my brain that it not only makes that racquetball sound but also goes in the wrong direction. I barely turn back in time to see it head straight for Bex at the speed of a freight train and hit her right in the gut.

"Oof." Bex doubles over, clutching her stomach.

"Oh, sugar monkeys!" Peyton calls out, her hands flying to cover her mouth.

I rush to Bex. "Are you okay? I am so sorry." How bad did I hurt her? I can tell I hit the ball hard, but I have no idea how much damage it might have caused. "Is it going to leave a bruise?"

Bex stands up straight, a mischievous smile on her face,

and holds up the ball. "Roman, these things weigh less than one ounce. I am *fine*." She laughs and presses the ball into my chest. My hand instinctively goes to it, landing right on top of hers.

"I see how it is," I say. "You helped me cover up one awkward moment by eclipsing it with another."

"I do what I can." She winks, and my heart might *flutter* just a bit. As she walks back to her position on the court, she asks, "Should we try again, and this time you hold back just a bit?"

"I *was* holding back." If only she knew how much I'm holding back with her.

"That was you *holding back*?" She looks straight at the camera. "Okay, then I want to see what it looks like when you *aren't* holding back. Toss me the ball and go to the other side of the court."

I do, and when I near Peyton, I say quietly, "I apologize for making a wrong assumption."

"Oh, my life, it's really no problem. But if you don't mind, I'm just going to..." Peyton points to the side of the court, and both she and Max head there.

Hit it like racquetball, I tell myself as Bex drops the ball and hits it with her paddle before ducking off to the side. It comes at me perfectly, and I take aim and swing like I'm playing hard with my buddy Kirk and I'm down by a handful of points. My racquet makes contact, the hit sounds completely unlike racquetball, and the ball hurtles straight for the chain-link wall surrounding the court. It hits one of the upright poles and falls to the ground.

Bex walks over to the ball, which now more closely

resembles an orange peel that someone has managed to get off the orange in one piece. "Will you look at that," she says as she takes the evidence of my misjudgment over to the camera. "That is *thoroughly destroyed!* I think that signals the end of the game. This guy can definitely liven up a game of pickleball, so make sure you check out his apps."

Her chosen profession might not be my thing, but I have to admire how good she is at it. Just seeing how comfortable she is in front of the camera and how it feels like she is talking to actual people when she is looking at nothing more than the camera lens is impressive.

"And make sure you subscribe and hit the bell for notifications because you won't want to miss my next interview with Roman. It's going to be at a location he doesn't even know yet, and I can tell you right now that you won't want to miss it."

I notice that Peyton and Max have come right up behind me, and they wave to the camera as Bex says goodbye to her Bexlandians.

As soon as the camera is off, I say, "I didn't mean to end the game."

"We already got what we needed, and we were losing good light, anyway. Not to mention the fact that my sister is in the parking lot, waiting to take my cameraman to basketball practice." She turns to Enoch and accepts the camera equipment from him, giving him a fist bump. "Thanks for another awesome job."

"And thank *you* for an awesome job." He takes a few steps toward the gate to let himself out of the court, then he turns, walking backward. "Oh, can I get paid differently this time?"

"Sure. You finally want cash?"

"No." Enoch makes a face like that's ridiculous. "I was thinking bacon burgers."

Bex laughs. "You got it."

"We are going to head out, too," Peyton says, and she and Max start walking to the parking lot.

I know enough about cameras to know that their owner prefers to be the one carrying them, so I offer to take the tripod. She hands it over, and we walk toward the gate. "I'm sorry I ruined the ball."

"Don't be. That made for some great viewing—my subscribers are going to love it." She looks me up and down, and I try to hold back the involuntary flex several of my muscles try to do just from seeing her notice. I try to hold back the smile, too. "I think a lot of them have been hoping to see those muscles in action. The rest will see it as evidence of the passion you bring to the things you take on."

I nod. "Well, I am sorry I hit you in the stomach with it."

"I wasn't joking when I said it was nothing."

I sneak a glance over at her while we walk. Amazingly, it doesn't matter what she wears, or if her hair is down, in a ponytail, perfect, or messed up from playing hard in a pickleball game, she's beautiful. Confident. In control. Unstoppable.

She must feel my eyes on her because a smile lifts the corners of her mouth.

The sun has just set but it's still plenty light outside. She leads us to her car, which is parked next to a row of shrubs on the driver's side. She opens the door to the backseat and lays down the camera case, then accepts the tripod from me and lays it beside the camera before shutting the door. I probably should say goodbye and walk away, but instead, as she's opening the driver's door, I lean against the car and ask, "So when will the first interview air?"

She turns so she's facing me—just the two of us nestled in the little space between her car and the shrubs, the open door behind her. "Next Tuesday. The same day your app releases."

"And you're going to show me before it airs, right?"

She gives me an amused smile that makes my chest tingle. "I always keep my word."

"So, are we talking five minutes before it airs, or with enough time to request changes?"

There's that same smile again, but she moves forward just a bit. Enough to make it feel like she wants the distance between us to close just as much as I do. "I will send it to you by Sunday evening so you'll have all day Monday to look at it."

I nod and turn so that I'm facing her fully, which puts me a little closer to her.

"We need to film the third one." Her eyes search mine. "When are you free?"

"Tomorrow," I say without thinking and instantly regret it. I don't want to tip my hand and show how much or how soon I want to see her again. So I add a quick, "Or next week," so it doesn't seem like I'm desperate.

"Tomorrow is perfect."

"Yeah?"

"Yeah." She moves a bit closer, and her eyes flick from mine to my lips. One slight little flick of her eyes, and suddenly all I can think about is her lips and how it would feel to kiss them. "Can you meet me at the inn?"

"Anywhere."

"Anywhere?"

I breathe out a chuckle and think, *As long as you're there.* Instead of answering, I just close the gap by a few more inches, and she's near enough that I can hear her soft breathing.

"I'm suddenly feeling drunk with the possibility of getting you to meet me anywhere."

I'm pretty sure she could talk me into anything right now. I reach out and run my fingers down her upper arm. She responds by touching her fingertips to my chest, and tingles spread up my spine as she starts to close the gap, her eyes on my lips.

"Bex!" Peyton yells as she runs around the bushes that separate where we are from the rest of the parking lot. "I'm so glad I caught you! Oh. *Oh!* My lands, I'm sorry. I didn't think I'd be interrupting… I just…" She opens the front passenger's door and tosses a bag inside. "I was afraid of leaving this in Max's car. I'll just…go now. Ignore me. Pretend I was never here."

Peyton races off, and we hear a car door shut and then the sound of Max's car driving off. Bex looks around like she's just come out of a daze. The moment is gone, though— I can see it in her eyes. I take a deep breath to pull myself out of the daze, too, and rub the back of my neck. "What time do you want me to meet you tomorrow night?"

"Oh, um, seven-thirty?"

I nod then turn and walk toward my car. It's probably a good thing we didn't actually kiss. What was I thinking? We're in a fairy tale world, not the real world. I'm reaching into my pocket to pull out my keys when Bex says, "Roman?"

I turn back toward her, not sure what, exactly, I'm hoping for, but knowing hope is very much alive and well.

"What was your favorite ice cream as a kid?"

That's not what I was expecting at all. "Uh, chocolate chip cookie dough."

She gives a nod and a wink, and then says, "See you tomorrow night."

Yep. Hope is definitely alive and well.

CHAPTER 11
Bex

THE TEXT COMES in from Ian's grandma, Shirley, next door. The woman has discovered the beauty of voice-to-text, but not how to edit what it thinks she said. Luckily, I'm practically a pro at translating voice-to-text. I have Vivian as a sister, after all. I type a quick response.

I get three eggs out of the fridge and head next door, breathing in the sweet afternoon air as I go. I started off the day by filming a *Hidden Inn Roomies* segment about the chaos of a morning when living in an inn full of entrepreneurs.

Peyton has been organizing bowls, mixers, food items, pots, pans, and containers to put the food in for a family she's making a week's worth of food. Timini has a play she's creating all the costumes for, and not only has she taken all six smaller tables in the dining area, but she's duking it out with Peyton over use of the dining table during the day, too. And all while Addison, Ian, and I are trying to grab something for breakfast before the three of us take half a dozen trips out to Addison's car to load up a ridiculous number of organization bins and other items for one of her clients.

Not long after Addison and Ian both leave, while Peyton and Timini are still discussing how to share the space, all of my sisters show up to film a *Sterling Sisters* segment. Then, once we finish, I figure I'll film my review of a stylish sports bag that a company sent me since Nikki can stay to film it. Enoch is my favorite cameraman, but since Nikki does most of the editing, she has a good feel for what, exactly, we need.

Filming always gives me a boost of energy. But now that it's late afternoon, all that extra energy is gone, and I'm crashing. The fresh air and time away from my computer help, though. I go straight to Shirley's kitchen door and knock twice before opening it.

"Oh, thank you," Shirley says as she turns from a bowl of something she's mixing on the counter and accepts the eggs from me. Her apron is covered in flour, and Carol, who is also wearing a flour-covered apron and stirring a bowl of something, sits at the kitchen table.

"What are you making?"

Shirley points at a muffin tin and a cake pan on the stove, the bowl in front of her, and the bowl in front of Carol. "Cookies, lemon tarts, and fudge jumbles. Our entire origami club district is getting together tonight."

"Wow! You guys really know how to party it up."

Carol stands, grabs a spoon from the drawer, and then scoops up a bit of the yellow substance in her bowl and hands it to me. "Here. Try this lemon curd."

I sit at the table, too, and put the spoon in my mouth. The curd is an explosion of flavor on my tongue—tart and sweet and so very lemony—and my eyes roll as I close them to savor every bit of it. "Oh, my, Carol." I lick the spoon. "This is divine. I can't speak for Addison, since she owns it, but if you two ever want to move into the inn, I'm sure we would all welcome you with open arms. And open mouths."

Both women laugh and go back to working on their sweet confections.

"So, tell me about who you're dating," Shirley says. "You know how much I love to live vicariously through your dating life."

"I actually haven't gone out with anyone in weeks."

"What? That isn't like you at all." Shirley grabs the bowl of dough she's mixing and brings it to the table, sitting down where she can face me. "What's going on?"

She's right. It isn't like me at all to not be dating. I always have at least one date a week. Quite often two or three. I love dating and am still convinced that if I date enough, I'll eventually find the right guy. How haven't I noticed that I'm not going on my usual number of dates?

"I guess I just haven't been looking lately."

Carol reaches a hand out and places it on my forehead. "Hmm. No fever. Strange. Are you feeling any other symptoms? Like maybe your mind just went for a walk without you?"

I laugh. "My mind and I are just fine." I think about it for a moment. "I guess maybe my mind has just been on Roman too much lately."

Shirley pushes the bowl she's been stirring to the side, like it's getting in the way of her listening to me, and leans forward, elbow on the table, chin in her palm. "This is the hottie you're interviewing for the Eddie Award judging thing, right? Are you thinking about dating him?"

"I'm not sure. I hadn't planned to at all, but maybe? All I know is that we came *this* close to kissing last night, and let's just say I wouldn't have been upset if we had." In fact, I can directly attribute all of my over-scheduling for the day to my need to stop thinking about that moment next to my car with Roman. The expression on his face. The way it felt when he touched my arm and when I touched his chest. How unguarded he was. The way his eyes were alive and warm and definitely wanting the kiss. The way he smelled. How great it felt to be so close and how much I wanted to step into his arms.

Carol hoots.

A satisfied grin spreads across Shirley's face. "When do you see him next?"

"Tonight. We're filming the third interview at the inn."

"And is this kiss that almost was going to happen then?"

I let out a long breath and look down at my arms, which are crossed and resting on the table, pondering. "I don't know. He's just the wrong type of guy for me. Normally, I have no fears dating, because if it doesn't work out, there are more fish in the sea, you know?"

I look up at the wiser, more experienced eyes across the table from me. "But Roman is just...different. This is the first time I've felt afraid. Like part of me knows that if I fall for him and it doesn't work out—which it won't—then I'm going to get hurt. I'm not just going to be able to shrug it off and go for the next fish in the sea like usual."

Shirley nods. "He's special, that one."

"Yep."

"Are you sure he's the wrong type of guy?" Carol asks.

"Well, yeah. He's very much unlike the type of guy I always date."

"That doesn't mean he's the wrong guy."

"Well, no, but I date the types of guys that I do because I've learned by watching my sisters what happens when you do and what happens when you don't. And I don't ever want to have to go through what my sister, Nikki, did."

Carol stands and carries the lemon curd to the mini crusts on the stove. "Open yourself to possibilities, girl. I thought my Henry was the wrong guy, and so did every person in my family. Once I took a flamethrower to that thought so I could see what lay beyond my preconceived notions, I stepped right over its ashes and into a beautiful life with him. We got to spend fifty-five years together before he passed a few months ago."

"Sounds like you need to get a flamethrower, dear," Shirley says.

I chuckle. "I will definitely think about your advice, Carol." I stand. "I better get back, though. I've got a lot to do to prepare for our interview tonight."

And one of those might just be getting a metaphorical thought-scorching flamethrower.

———

I peek through the blinds on the gathering room window to the curved driveway in front of the inn. The moment I see Roman's car pull in, giddiness sweeps through me. "He's here!" I say to Enoch. He turns on the camera, and we both go to the front lobby.

As soon as Roman knocks, I open the door and say, "Hi."

His eyes immediately go to the camera. "Oh. We're starting off with the camera on, then?"

"I want to make sure I get on film your reaction to seeing where I am interviewing you."

He looks wary, so I open the door all the way, grab his hand, and pull him toward the gathering room, using my foot to shut the door behind us. Enoch moves from behind us to the side so he can film at a good angle.

The second Roman walks through the doorway and his eyes land on the gigantic blanket fort that Addison, Peyton, Timini, Ian, Enoch, and I built, they go wide, and it is worth every bit of struggle we had to get it to work. I don't remember the task being so difficult when I was a kid.

Of course, when I was a kid, our family room was less than one-third of the size of this huge room, and we were never as ambitious when it came to fort size as my room-mates and I were tonight. Enoch had set up the camera back between the area with the couches at the front of the room and my desk at the back when we first started building the blanket fort. It will likely make for some great time-lapse footage, and if I want to post some bloopers at the end, we definitely had plenty of those.

"Oh, wow. You didn't. I can't believe—" Roman runs a hand down his face like he's wiping away any chance that this is a mirage. "It's been so long."

I look at the camera. "In our pre-interview, Roman said that one of his favorite things to do as a kid was to eat ice cream in blanket forts that he made with his brothers, so I figured it would be a great place to chat with him today."

I lead him to the opening and we crawl inside, Enoch right behind us. We used practically every blanket and sheet we collectively own, so surrounding us is quite the colorful tapestry. We put the cushions from all three couches on the floor, too, so we have soft places to sit. And, because I know how important it is, I have some great lighting set up that will allow my viewers to see everything yet still have that feel of being in a cave made of blankets. I added a few flashlights pointing at the blanket walls since that's the kind of lighting that completes the look.

I show Roman where to sit, then I take my seat on my mark and Enoch gets the camera into position.

Roman looks around at the area, which feels like one larger room and three smaller ones. One area is even like a hallway leading to another section. "The dress forms aren't bad, but those mannequins are really freaking me out."

I laugh as I look at the shiny white mannequins, standing like a mix between a pillar holding up our fort and a ghost wearing a blanket like a shawl. It doesn't help that their arms are positioned outward and up to help hold up the fort because now that I'm on the floor looking up at them, they appear more than a little menacing. "It's hard to come up with enough tall objects to hold up the blankets. Timini offered these, and I think they really add to the look of the place."

"Yep. They add to the look of it being haunted." He keeps glancing at the closest one like it can't be trusted, which makes me laugh out loud. And it makes Enoch keep taking his eyes off the video camera and looking at it like he's just as wary.

I start with an introduction of Roman, just in case people are watching who haven't seen either of the other two interviews, and I ask Roman a few questions about his company.

"Wow," I say after hearing him talk about it. "It sounds like you've put together a pretty stellar group of employees."

He smiles in a way that tells me he's really proud of them, and I can't help but just stare at his beautiful face for a moment. His beautiful, strong-jawed, perfectly-stubbled, melt-your-heart face. Then I realize that I'm just staring at that face for far too long to be a proper interview and clear my throat.

"You have an app that has been a fan favorite for quite a while now, right? I want to hear more about it."

"The one that made us famous is *Musicbound*. Think of the last movie you watched. Now imagine it without any music. No soundtrack at all."

I flinch, just thinking of how wrong that feels. And for some reason, it makes Enoch look at the mannequin closest to him like if he doesn't keep an eye on it, it's going to attack him or something.

"Music adds a lot to a movie. We thought book reading should be the same, so we created an app to provide music while you're reading an ebook or listening to an audiobook. The app will scan the book and look for subjects, themes, tone, and a couple dozen more metrics. Then it'll select music to play while you read that fits the feel and the plot of the book. In chapters where something sad happens, the music will be more somber. When it's an action-packed scene, the music will be upbeat and fast. Just like in the movies, it'll fit what you are reading."

"Shut the front door." I look at the camera, knowing that if my viewers aren't already using this app, they are going to be just as stunned by this as I am. "Are you kidding me right now? This is really a thing?"

Roman's smile is wide.

"If you re-read a book, will the music be the same the next time?"

"Not necessarily. If you read the same book a year later, there will be more songs that have been put out into the world, so it might choose one of those. And if you're a slower reader, you'll hear more songs than the faster readers."

I put my hands up and jerk back a bit, like I've been hit by a blast. "How do I not already have this in my life?" I take my phone out of my pocket and open the app store. "I need this right now. This purple one with the music note on a book is it, right?"

"Yep."

As it's downloading, I look out at my viewers. "Did you all already know about this? If so, why didn't you tell me? And if you haven't already told everyone you know about this, you should do it the second you finish watching this video." Then I turn back to Roman. "Does it work with nonfiction?"

He makes a motion with his head that is both a nod and a shake. "We designed it to work with fiction books only. I still use it with every nonfiction book I read, though. I've gotten some interesting results. It has made me double my nonfiction reading just to hear what kind of music it chooses for it."

"Give me an example."

"Let me think. Oh. Okay. I was reading B.J. Fogg's *Tiny Habits*, and one of the songs it played was *Hard Habit to Break* by Chicago. And while I was reading *Deep Work* by Cal Newport, it played a bunch of music that was scientifically proven to help with focus like classical music, nature sounds, and binaural beats."

"Impressive."

"I thought so, too. My favorite, though, was when I was reading *Year of Yes* by Shonda Rhimes. During one chapter, it played Kelly Clarkson's *What Doesn't Kill You Makes You Stronger*, and in another chapter, Katy Perry's *Roar*."

I laugh, feeling like they are some pretty appropriate choices, and Roman's eyes shine with a mix of pride, satisfaction, and enjoyment. I feel like I'm seeing through to the real him. And he read *Year of Yes*! My heart melts even more to know that he read a book by a woman who is all about creating shows that people can connect to. Maybe I've misjudged Roman and the way he feels about my job.

Instead of continuing to stare at him, my jaw still hanging at the revelations like I've lost all ability to control it, I look down at the app on my phone. "It feels like such a shame that this app has been out in the world and I haven't been using it."

"At least you have it now."

"Yes. This calls for a celebration." I twist to grab the mini cooler that I snuggled between a couch cushion and a blanket to my side and open it up. I pull out a couple of pints of Ben & Jerry's and two spoons and hand one to Roman. "Half-baked for the app genius, and Red, White, and Blueberry for the giddy new app owner."

We both take off our lids and scoop up a spoonful of ice cream. Roman closes his eyes and savors his bite, and I wonder how long it has been since he's eaten ice cream. Or at least a flavor of ice cream that reminds him of his child-hood. He puts a hand behind him and leans back, stretching his legs forward.

The blanket fort is definitely much larger than a kid's version. But we aren't kids—we are two adults and a twelve-year-old who is as tall as I am and bigger or not, this place is still cozy. And Roman's legs are long. So when he stretches, they bump the base of the mannequin that Enoch has been most wary of.

Enoch flinches in surprise when he notices the movement from the corner of his eye, then jerks in fear as the mannequin wobbles, looking like it has come to life. In an instant, he is scuttling backward, the couch cushion he's sitting on and the blanket tucked under the edge of it going with him.

"No!" I shout as I instinctively lunge forward to grab hold of the mannequin that is now falling forward as the weight of the blanket resting on its head is being tugged, and

Roman instinctively lunges over me to protect me from above. I grab the mannequin by its hard plastic ankles—not that it helps at all—just as it falls to the ground.

Then, like dominos, all of the mannequins and dress forms fall to the ground, all the blankets being pulled down on top of them.

And suddenly, I am in a very dark, very muffled, very small space, looking up at Roman, whose hands are on the floor, one next to each of my shoulders, the only space between us made by the length of his arms from wrist to shoulder as he hovers over me. He's currently the only thing holding up any part of the fort.

"Impressive save," I breathe.

He shifts his knees, and I let go of my grip on the mannequin's ankle that I realize my right hand is still clutching.

"This isn't quite how I remember blanket forts as a kid."

"What, you never had mannequins attack you in yours?"

He chuckles, and even though I can't see his face, I can sense exactly the way his mouth is tugged up on one side and how his eyes are twinkling. He is so close that I can feel his breath on my cheek, feel the warmth of his body emanating from him. "I don't suppose you know the best direction to head to find our way out?"

"Out?" I reach up and touch my fingertips to his cheek. I'm not sure I want to get out anytime soon.

CHAPTER 12
Roman

The feel of Bex's fingers on my cheek sends a thrill racing to every corner of my body. All I can think about is kissing her. She is right there, inches from me. I'd just have to bend my elbows a bit, and my lips could be on hers.

Is that what she wants? As her fingers run along my jawline and pause at my chin, her breath catching, her fingers tapping twice lightly, I think maybe so.

"I finally found you!" Enoch's face appears under the blanket next to us, a flashlight in one hand and the video camera in the other. He lets out a huge breath of air. "Whew. That wasn't easy. I swear the mannequin was still trying to attack me."

Now that I can see Bex's face, I see amusement. We both shift to where we are on our hands and knees and work our way to a spot where the blankets have pulled apart and we can see light. Once we make our way out, Bex runs her hands over her hair, which is looking rather staticy from all the blankets rubbing on it, and straightens her shirt. I do the same, figuring I probably need it as much as she does.

She surveys the damage as Enoch pans the camera around at the destruction. With her hands on her hips and the camera focused on her, she says, "Well, as is the eventual outcome of all blanket forts, this one has crumbled under the weight of its own greatness—just a little sooner than we had planned." She reminds her viewers about subscribing, getting notifications, and not missing our next interview, and then we both say goodbye.

I bend down, pick up a blanket, and start folding it. She gives me a strange look like she hadn't expected me to help, but then she grabs the other side of the blanket and starts folding it with me. I'm not about to leave this big mess to her, though. Even if my mom hadn't taught me to always show good manners, I'd want to stay and help just to be around her for longer.

She gasps. "The ice cream!"

"I've got this," Enoch says, dropping the blanket he's folding before making a show of diving into the pile of blankets. A minute later, he re-emerges holding two pints of ice cream and two spoons. "Only a little bit got on the hardwood floor—none on the cushions or the blanket." He looks at the pints in his hand. "Are you going to still eat these?"

Bex laughs. "Consider it your reward for rescuing them."

"Yes!"

Then the kid rushes over to Bex's desk and starts eating them at a speed that pretty much guarantees brain freeze. I shake my head. Enoch is impressively professional behind the camera, but he is still a twelve-year-old boy.

Once we get the blankets folded, the ice cream cleaned off the floor, and the furniture put back into place, Bex walks me out to my car.

"Thank you, Bex. Even with the fort crashing down on us, I quite enjoyed myself. That wasn't something I thought I would do again anytime soon." When she didn't tell me what we were going to do for this interview, my mind had been churning, trying to figure it out. It hadn't occurred to me that she would create an entire blanket fort. Climbing inside it brought back so much nostalgia.

"And thank you for being game for it. Now tell me, Roman Powell, when you were a kid, what was it about blanket forts that was so magical to you?"

It's dark outside yet the moon is bright enough that I can see the same look on her face that she gets whenever she is filming. Like she experiences her own kind of magic every time she has the camera on her.

We reach my car and I lean my backside against it, trying to remember back to what I loved so much about the forts we made. "I guess part of it was that we only made them when my dad was away on a business trip, which always meant that our schedules were less rigid. And the other part was the games my brothers and I would play in it. More often than not, we played business owner and employees."

"Was that really what you played?"

I chuckle and look down, shaking my head. "That's what we called it, even. I was always the business owner since I was the oldest, and I got to boss my brothers around."

"I see why it was your favorite game."

"My dad likes to control everything. So I guess a big part

of why we loved it was that we could make all the decisions ourselves without our dad stepping in to tell us what to do." It has never occurred to me before that in my business, I walked right into a situation that, as a kid, I had worked to stay away from.

"Well, it looks like all that practice being a business owner as a kid really paid off."

She is so beautiful. And I really want to kiss her. But then a look crosses her face that makes me think that she's unsure about it. Or flat-out doesn't want to kiss me at all. I am, after all, just a stuffy businessman, which seems to be her least favorite type of person.

I need to convince her that I am right for her. She steps closer to me, and my chest lifts at the thought that maybe the moment we shared under the collapsed blanket fort hasn't been lost.

But then, just as I am thinking about how much I want to close the gap between us, a car pulls into the driveway, and I want to curse its driver. Its headlights shine on us, and Bex takes a step back, turning toward it with her hand shielding her eyes from its lights. "Oh. That's my sister, Kenna, here to pick up Enoch."

I hope that Enoch will see that she pulled up and run out to the car. But her sister pulls to a stop just in front of me on the curved drive and gets out. "Hey, Bex! Can I grab those frames you picked up for me?"

"Yeah. Just…" Bex meets my eyes and then turns back to her sister. "Go on in, and I'll be right there."

As soon as Kenna is inside the inn, Bex turns to me.

"Sorry about the interruption. I believe you were about to tell me I'm pretty."

"And talented and a fairly solid blanket fort maker. And I believe you were about to tell me that I'm devilishly handsome."

"And a natural on camera—when you let your guard down—and an excellent kisser."

I quirk an eyebrow and drink in the brilliant smile on her face. "I know you have a rule of not endorsing products you haven't personally tried. I think I better help you to not break that rule."

"Don't let anyone ever tell you that you only look out for your own interests."

This time, I move toward her. We are standing so close. The air between us feels alive with electricity. A warmth. Like it's buzzing in anticipation. I feel the same buzz in me as I feel the warmth of her breath on my neck as she looks up at me.

We are only inches apart when I hear a meow and look down to see that a cat is rubbing up against Bex's leg, then forcing herself into the space between us.

"Skittles, go back home," Bex says. "I don't have any food for you, but I bet Carol does."

I shake my head. First her roommate, Peyton, interrupts us at the pickleball courts. Then Enoch in the blanket fort. Then her sister Kenna. And now the neighbor's cat. "Except it seems as though the universe is conspiring against us kissing."

Bex closes what's left of the distance between us and

moves her hands up to either side of my face. "Then we need to show the universe who's boss," she breathes. She meets my eyes for a moment, then, like she's afraid something else will stop us if she doesn't hurry and seize the moment, she brings her lips to mine. They're firm and smooth, and they somehow feel like they're a perfect match to mine.

My spine tingles, and I wrap my arms around her waist, pulling her closer, loving the feel of her body against mine. I have never kissed someone so strong and decisive before, and her kiss is every bit as powerful as she is, seeming to shake me to my core. I break from the kiss just enough to whisper, "You are amazing," my lips brushing against hers with the words before they meet her lips again.

She moves her fingertips to just behind my neck, sending a new wave of tingles across my back. After a few blissful moments of her lips moving against mine, she pulls back slightly, a small moan escaping her lips. "Roman, that was… Wow. You really know how to kiss a girl."

I'm pretty sure the magic of that kiss is all from her. "Go on a date with me. No cameras, no interviews, just you and me."

"Just you and me?"

I nod.

She gives me one more slow kiss on the lips. "I would love that." She looks up, biting her lip like she's thinking through things, and it makes me want to kiss her again. "I have a pretty full schedule this weekend to prepare for the start of judging on Monday. Are you free next Thursday?"

I nod. "I'll pick you up at seven."

I get the last of the things I need for the day's meetings organized and into folders with a smile on my face and a lightness in my chest. I love the release day of a new app more than any other day—even more than the high we all get when we brainstorm a concept we know will be a winner. Even more than the day we work through the final issue and get it ready to go live. Release day is the day when we get to see what users think of the product we've poured everything into.

But that isn't the only thing giving me a bounce in my step. I wake up Monday morning realizing that I actually enjoy my interviews with Bex. Maybe because the first three were filmed with only a couple of days in between, but I have to wait a full eight days between the third and fourth. It gives me time to realize how much I want the next one to come.

My first interview with Bex goes live this morning, too. I never would've guessed I'd enjoy creating those videos with her, but there's something exhilarating about putting myself out there and having people respond. It oddly feels similar to putting a new app out there. I have given a part of myself to both, yet once either is released into the world, it feels separate from me. Almost like at that point, it's something that belongs to the viewers and app users, no longer to me, to Bex, or to my company.

Doing the interviews with Bex has also been oddly free-ing. Opening myself up a bit and letting strangers get to know me comes with plenty of people who aren't bashful about criticizing. But more people respond positively. It makes me feel like there will always be people who will accept me no matter what. I don't need to be so guarded and careful. Maybe I'll have to say yes to interviews more often.

Another thing that surprises me is how much I enjoy the way Bex gets me to open up a bit more. It leaves me waking up each day more excited than I have possibly been, ever.

But maybe part of it is the creative ways I've been able to find to see and talk with Bex between our third interview on Thursday when we kissed and today.

I walk into my nine a.m. department heads meeting. Since it's release day for Nudge Out, it's Everly's meeting. I'm not surprised to see a giant cake in the middle of the conference table and several groups of balloons in the green and blue of the Nudge Out icon placed in groups around the room. My team has worked hard on this—they deserve to celebrate. We all do.

Everly opens the meeting by giving the release day numbers of app downloads—which are, by far, the best release numbers we've ever had, even though our advertising budget hasn't been much different from the last one. There's quite a bit of high-fiving and cheering all around the room.

"And I think a good part of those numbers came from the interview released early this morning that our illustrious leader did with Bex Sterling on *Bexlandia*." She meets my eyes. "Can I show it to them?"

It's nice of her to ask my permission, even though we both know there's no way the rest of my team is going to let me leave without it being shown. So I give the okay.

In all the time between when we filmed the hour-long interview and today, I've thought back through everything that happened. Sure, there were some exciting parts, but I worry the video will be slow and boring and no one will hang around for the exciting parts. But when Bex sent it to me on Sunday, just like she promised, and I watched it for the first time, I was surprised at how well-edited and well-paced it was.

The part with the deer staring us down right before it decides to charge makes me laugh, and now that I'm watching with my team, I smile at how much it makes them laugh, too.

If I were the one who'd fallen into the stream while being chased by the deer, though, I wouldn't have wanted it in the video. I'm impressed that Bex includes it. She was right— letting the viewers see all of that kind of stuff definitely makes the whole thing more interesting. And I get why it helps her audience connect with her more.

For so long, I had anticipated having multiple things in the video that I wasn't okay with including and possibly having to use threats to get Bex to edit them out. As it turned out, I didn't ask her to change a thing. I enjoy the email thread going back and forth to tell her that, though. I can't say I've ever flirted so much over email before.

As the video finishes and Everly takes it off the main screen, all my department heads cheer and it makes me feel a bit like a rock star. I'm enjoying this a bit too much.

"Now that's what I call good marketing," Wells says. "That's going to be giving us a boost for a while."

Daran chuckles. "Much like what that deer was trying to do to you."

"You guys don't plan on letting me live that down, do you?"

"Not anytime soon," Everly says, her eyebrows pulling together as she scrolls through something on her laptop. "So far, it looks like almost everything in the comments is positive. Lots of people are saying that they just downloaded the app, or coming back to say they got it and are so excited to use it."

"I bet those investors are going to love this," Melinda says.

I hope so. I'm having a meeting with them in a couple of weeks—long enough away that a few of the interviews will be out. I'll be surprised if this doesn't give them everything they need.

Everly gasps and puts a hand to her mouth. She stays silent, though, still reading. Finally, she looks up at me. "They're shipping you!"

I shake my head, having no clue what she's talking about.

"Shipping," she repeats, enunciating the word. "You and Bex."

"Everly, I heard you fine. I still don't know what you mean."

"Ship, as in relation*ship*. It means they want the two of you to start dating! Oh my gosh, that is so cute." She reads a little more. "Her viewers practically worship her. And whatever they saw during that video in her and whatever they saw in you made them think that the two of you should be together."

I don't know what I think about that. Part of me is completely unsettled that strangers are weighing in on who I should date. But as much as Bex has been on my mind lately, I like hearing that they can tell she's feeling it, too.

And it makes me want to win her over even more. Just two more days, and we're going on a date. I'm going to make sure it's perfect.

CHAPTER 13

Bex

I AM GOING to murder my sisters. All four of them. Starting with Vivian. Sure, Vivian says no to Asher getting a bird, but she doesn't say no to him signing up for *Forty Winks with Feathered Friends* camp. And then I am going to murder Kenna, Nikki, and Fiona for goading me, saying how good it will be for me to face my fears and maybe even overcome them. I am now quite convinced that science doesn't support that theory. Quite the opposite, in fact.

And while I'm at it, I'm going to murder the heart attack that killed Vivian's husband's great uncle Roger, because it makes it so Vivian can't take her own son to the mother-son event, and I have to step in.

"Just make a video for your channel of you overcoming your fears," they said. "It'll be inspiring to your viewers."

And I fell for it.

Even though I'm pretty sure that Nikki is just pushing for me to have this "opportunity" so that she can be the one at

Vivian's house, sleeping over in a nice, soft bed, while watching the other three kids, instead of out here, under the stars, on a creaky cot with nothing more than a sleeping bag protecting me from the elements.

And by "elements," I mean the vile winged creatures.

I made it through the evening's events. I am proud of how strong I've been, actually. We studied the nests of birds and then built our own; watched a live show where they demonstrated the movement of birds as they dove, soared, waddled, strutted, and glided; learned enough facts about birds to make me even more wary of them; and went on a treasure hunt for the kinds of things birds like to eat. If nothing else, I did get some priceless footage.

But now it's after two in the morning, and even though I'm surrounded by a bunch of parents and bird-obsessed seven-to-ten-year-olds who are spread out across the pavilion, all in their own sleeping bags on cots, all sleeping, I haven't been able to close my eyes for more than a few seconds at a time. Birds are everywhere. Sure, some are behind a netted fence, but a lot of them are right here with us. Where they can just walk right up to us or land on our heads.

One, in particular, is as tall as a good-sized dog and apparently nocturnal, because it isn't tucked away sleeping somewhere—it's watching me. Not like, *Oh, she's something interesting to watch for a bit.* More like, *I'm going to wait for her to drop her guard long enough to fall asleep, and then I'm going to swoop in and peck her face.*

For the millionth time, I think about calling Nikki to see if we can switch places—her husband is easy-going enough that he'd be supportive. But sleeping on a cot is probably not the best thing for a pregnant belly. And, duh, neither of us can leave the sleeping kids in our care alone while we swap places.

I can't call any of my sisters, really. Not after how much grief they've given me about facing my fears. Besides, what I've filmed for my channel is great, and I know my audience will love it. So of course I want to air it. But if I don't see this through, I'll feel like I'm not being honest and authentic with them. Obviously, I can't do that. Besides, it's good to let my viewers know when I struggle with things and still overcome. So I will overcome.

Maybe.

Or maybe not.

All signs are pointing to *not*.

I suddenly feel hot, and like I can't breathe. And my legs won't stay still. I grab my phone and get out of my sleeping bag. I can't just lie here in such a vulnerable position any longer. If I'm going to get attacked, I want to be on my feet, ready to run, arms ready to flail. I shake out my hands— partly to shake away my fears, and partly to make sure they're ready for the imminent flailing. Then I fold my arms and rub them with my hands. It's a little chilly to be outside of my sleeping bag.

I have to stop thinking about the birds. I'm never going to sleep if I can't get them out of my mind. I just don't know how to accomplish that.

Oh! *Memes*. Nikki sent me a bunch made by viewers that are related to my first video interview with Roman that went live yesterday. I've been too busy to be online at all over the past day and a half, but Nikki assures me that she sent some good ones that are representative of what's out there. Maybe that will distract me. I open Messenger and start scrolling through Nikki's picks.

The first one is a zoomed-in screenshot of Roman's and my faces. By the terror in our expressions, I'm guessing it was the exact moment when we realized that the deer was going to charge, right before we turned to run. The words on the photo read:

When you write a cathartic email to your boss about his short-comings and accidentally click send.

I chuckle and shake my head. The one right below it is the same picture of our panicked faces, only the words say:

When the teacher says one minute left to take the test, and you realize there's a back side.

The next one is an image of us running from the deer. I'm still impressed that Enoch managed to get ahead of us enough to video Roman and me running away. The picture is blurry in spots, but the look on our faces and the speed that we're obviously running tells a story all on its own. As does the look of determination on the deer's face. The word *Me* is placed over Roman and me, and the words *My problems* are placed on the deer.

There is another one of the same picture, but this one says, *I don't always run away, but when I do, I run through the least accommodating terrain possible.* I nearly laugh out loud, but then remember everyone sleeping around me. Looking back at our interview, it probably would've made a lot more sense if we'd just stayed on the path and kept running toward our cars.

Then a third with that same picture, which makes me wonder how many more are out there. It reads *I think she wants to nudge them out of their comfort zone.* A snort escapes my mouth on that one. Roman would probably even laugh at it.

Aww. And then one that makes me smile. It has two pictures, side by side. One is of me, looking at Roman like I adore everything about him. I hadn't noticed ever making that face when I was going through the edited video, but you can find pretty much any face on a person in a video if you press pause at just the right moment. The second picture is of Roman holding out a hand to pull me up when I'd fallen into the creek. The only words on the post are the hashtag *#RelationshipGoals*.

The last three are all the same animated gif—of me slipping in the water and falling flat on my back, the two-second clip repeating over and over. The first has the caption *How my life is going.* The next says, *Me, any time I walk past my crush.* And then the last one—*When I'm trying to look like a skilled professional and my boss is watching.*

I can tell which posts come from fans because they all seem to have the hashtag *#BexVsDeer*. I click on the hashtag and start scrolling through the posts it brings up. There are dozens of memes. No, hundreds. All with videos, animated gifs, or screenshot images of something that happened during that interview. And that's just on one social media platform, with this one tag. I can't imagine how many more are on every other platform.

The last one I see before closing out of the app is a

zoomed-in shot of the deer, with that murderous look in her eye. It says, *Say it to my face, bro. I deer you.*

Man, that deer really was creepy. Just looking into her eyes in a picture gives me a cold shiver.

And it very quickly reminds me of where I am and just as quickly alarms me. That had been one effective distraction to pull me from the danger of my surroundings. Now that I've been staring at my bright screen, my eyes are blind to the darkness, making it even more insidious. I aim the screen at the area in front of me, blinking to hopefully make myself focus more quickly.

The meager light shines on something in front of me, and I yelp and jump backward. The huge bird that had been watching me earlier has waddled over, quiet as a ninja, and is standing right at my feet, staring up at me. I suddenly find myself with my phone to my ear, listening to the ringing of my call to Roman.

Why am I calling him? I might not be willing to call one of my sisters, but I could've called any one of my roommates. Or even my mom or dad. But no—I call Roman.

I keep my eyes on the bird, hearing my own heartbeat pumping in my ears like an overly excited aerobics instructor. My chest is getting tighter, which is unfortunate because it gives less room for the battle going on between the wildebeests in my stomach. I jump at the sound of a rustling behind me, then roll my shoulders, darting my eyes around at everything.

"Bex?" Roman answers the phone groggily, his voice thick with sleep.

"Please tell me you know how to talk someone down from a phobia attack," I whisper in a voice that is bordering on hysterical, clutching the phone with both hands. My breaths are coming fast and I keep glancing around, making sure no other birds are trying to flank me and attack from behind, all while keeping an eye on the one right in front of me.

"Phobia attack? What's going on?"

"There is a bird right in front of me that I swear has been around since the dinosaurs. That's how big he is. He's got black feathers and black legs and even a black beak that—I am not kidding you—is as long as a butcher knife. Around his eyes and cheeks and a giant neck thing, though. That part's not black—it's bright orange. Like it's there just to remind you that he's unpredictable. I saw him earlier on the tour, and I'm pretty sure he's been plotting my demise ever since. He was awake then, so I'm pretty sure that means he's not actually nocturnal—he just made an exception for me. And Roman! He is following me! Every time I take a step, he takes a step."

"Where are you?" His voice sounds a little more awake but also more baffled.

I try to get further from the sleeping people so I won't wake them. Every step I take is matched by the cursed bird and I can't slow my breathing. "The aviary."

"Why are you at the aviary if you have a phobia of birds? And why at nearly three in the morning?"

I let out a huff of air. "Because I'm stupid. And a sucker for helping out with my nieces and nephews."

"Ahh," he breathes. "You're at the *Forty Winks with Feathered Friends* camp. I did that when I was a kid, too."

"What? *Why?* Are you a secret bird lover? I might have to cancel our last interview. And our date."

"You're not a fan of birds or people who like birds. Got it. I assume your nephew is exempt from your ire?"

I take my eyes off the bird long enough to glance over to where Asher lies sleeping in the cot next to mine. "Yes. Because he's eight and adorable." Then my eyes are back on the bird's, and I swear he's moved closer during that second my focus was away. "Roman, what do I do? He just keeps staring at me with those beady eyes. I'm pretty sure he can see right into my soul."

"He probably likes what he sees. That's why he's following you."

"Roman!" I hiss.

"Okay," he says, and I hear some rustling, like maybe he's adjusting to a seated position in bed. "Tell me why you're so afraid of birds."

"Because they've got grabby, stabby feet. And grabby, stabby beaks. And since they can fly, they can attack you from any direction." I duck, looking all around, suddenly worried about how many birds are waiting on top of the posts and buildings and light poles. "They swarm. And they carry diseases."

"They do not."

"And they're smart—you've seen them fly in formations. They're capable of planning a coordinated attack to take over the world."

"No, they aren't."

"Remember how I said that they're smart?"

"Okay, they're smart, but they wouldn't. They aren't vindictive like that."

"Ducks are."

"Okay, ducks are. But not that bird in front of you."

"How do you know? He looks smart *and* vindictive! And birds can't be trusted!"

"These birds can be trusted. Bex, the aviary has been doing this activity for years. Since long before I was old enough to go. They wouldn't have started it and definitely wouldn't continue it if they were worried about that happening. Or if anything bad had happened in all the years they've done it."

"Maybe this is a new bird. He keeps cocking his head as he's staring at me. Like he's planning something."

"He's not sizing you up for a meal, Bex. He's just curious. Birds aren't mean—they're just inquisitive. He's watching you because you're the only one who's awake. There's no one else to watch."

I look out across the pavilion. Everyone else is all snuggled in their sleeping bags, snoozing. Is he really only interested in me because I'm giving him a show to watch? "Are you sure?"

"Positive. Birds are social creatures. This one got up in the middle of the night, scratched his head as he was wandering to the refrigerator, and noticed the TV was on. So he thought, 'Hey, that show looks interesting. Pretty girl, too. I think I'll just plop down on the couch and watch for a bit as I eat this slice of pizza.'"

I let out a quiet laugh and feel some of the tension leaving my shoulders.

"If you go climb into your sleeping bag and close your eyes, the bird's going to go, 'Looks like this show is over, and the next one is boring. I might as well go back to bed.' Then he'll stumble his way back to his nest and totally forget it even happened by morning. Unless he notices the missing piece of pizza, of course."

"And the pepperoni morning breath."

"Definitely that."

I take a deep breath as the war in my stomach calms down to a half-hearted disagreement. I hadn't expected Roman to be so patient. Nikki's ex-husband hadn't been, that was for sure. Maybe I've been wrong about Roman, and he isn't like my old brother-in-law. Maybe he isn't so rigid and overbearing. Not only does he pick up the phone in the middle of the night, but he's understanding. And, actually, helpful. I feel my heart rate returning to normal. I open and close my hand, trying to ease the cramp from my death grip on the phone.

"It surprises me that you have a phobia. I thought nothing could faze you."

"And I didn't think you'd be so patient after being woken up in the middle of the night."

He lets out a chuckling breath, and I can hear the smile in it. "For what it's worth, I'm impressed you were willing to go to this thing with your nephew. That took guts."

"And a lot of razzing from my sisters." I walk back over to my cot and sit down on it.

He chuckles. "That's what siblings are for."

"You really think it's safe for me to go to sleep?" I whisper. I hope so because I am so very exhausted.

"I do."

"Thank you, Roman, for answering in the middle of the night and for talking me down."

There's a long pause before he says, "Thank you for trusting me to."

"I'll see you tomorrow at seven?"

"Tomorrow at seven." I can hear the smile in his voice.

I hang up the phone, and I hear Asher's cot creak as he lifts his head. "Was that your boyfriend? I heard you talking." His voice is so groggy I can barely make out the words.

"I don't have a boyfriend, silly." I reach out and ruffle Asher's hair.

"Not usually, but Roman isn't usual. He's special." Then his head hits his pillow again, and his breaths turn to the rhythmic breathing of sleep.

"He is," I whisper, and then snuggle into my own sleeping bag.

CHAPTER 14
Roman

I PLACE my hand on the small of Bex's back as I guide her toward the restaurant. Kitchen Seven Twelve is my favorite in Gresham, and I'm excited to share it with Bex. I want every part of this date to go perfectly. "Have I told you that you look beautiful tonight?" She's wearing a sky-blue dress that looks amazing with her skin tone and heels that show off her incredible legs.

Even though it's only the third day since Nudge Out was released and the number of downloads is exceeding all our expectations, causing a buzz of energy to constantly run through the office, I still somehow think about Bex more than anything else.

I've especially been unable to stop thinking about her since the moment she called me in the middle of the night last night. Sure, she'd been unreasonably afraid of the birds, but in light of the fear she had, she showed remarkable fortitude. I like a woman who stands courageous in the face of opposition. And I really like the fact that I'm the one she called to calm her fears. More than ever, it makes me want this date to go perfectly.

As soon as the guy at the hostess counter walks over to join the rest of his group, Bex and I step up to it. The woman behind the counter gives a wide smile. "Welcome. Do you have a reservation?"

I nod. "For Roman Powell, in the summer room." The summer room is one of the main reasons why I wanted to bring her to this restaurant specifically. It's a room tucked away in the corner with just one single table. The room is modern, simple, and tastefully decorated. It's the perfect place for us to just go and quietly chat while eating great food, without the chaos of a busy restaurant.

"Oh," the hostess says, her brows pulling together as she looks down at the schedule. She flips to a different page in the folder and then checks something on a tablet. "I am so sorry, sir. It appears that the room was double-booked."

I rub my temple. "When will it be available?"

The woman winces. "Not for about two hours. If you don't mind sitting in the main lobby, though, I can bump you to the front of the wait list and get you seated within just a couple of minutes."

I look at Bex.

"That's totally fine," she says.

So I nod at the woman, and, true to her word, she has us seated in under three minutes. It's not even at a booth—it's a table right in the middle of the room. I'm irritated, but when Bex reaches across the table and places her hand on my arm, my irritation flees.

"Your face looks as beautiful as ever. So I'm guessing there weren't any bird attacks once you fell asleep? You *did* fall asleep, right?"

"I did. And nope, no attacks. You were right—the big bird wandered away as soon as there was nothing to see."

"Presumably to his nest, where he would wake up with pizza breath."

Bex laughs. "I can only assume." She meets my eyes. "Thank you, again, for answering your phone last night."

I smile at her, gazing at those alluring eyes with the rim of gold around the outer edge.

"Since you got to witness my biggest phobia last night, I think it's only fair for you to share yours with me."

"Is that how it works?"

"Yep. By answering the phone last night and not hanging up once you heard my panicked voice, you were thereby agreeing to share your biggest fear tonight. It's all but a legally binding contract."

I raise an eyebrow and try to hold back a smile.

"So spill it."

"Okay. I have automatonophobia."

Bex narrows her eyes at me for a moment, then, instead of asking me what it is, she pulls her phone from her purse and looks it up. I can tell the moment she finds it because she gives me a flat look. "'A fear of human-like figures.' Like, say, of mannequins that are holding up a blanket fort right before they come crashing down on you?"

This time I laugh. The name of that phobia is one of the useless bits of information floating around in my head that I never thought would come in handy. Like knowing the first twenty digits of pi or that a day on Venus is longer than a year on Venus. But today, I'm grateful that little tidbit is in there.

She puts her phone back in her purse. "Okay, now I want the real one."

My biggest fear is probably being judged by my peers as being not good enough. But I'm not about to tell her that. Instead, I go for a fear that makes me feel foolish for sharing but won't make me feel completely exposed. "I have a fear of needles. And, interestingly enough, I don't know what that phobia is called."

"Needles? Huh. So what happens when you need to get blood drawn?"

"Well, I'm not a fan of looking like a wimp, so I just focus on not freaking out. Usually, it works, but every once in a while I..." I glance around the room, embarrassed that someone might hear, "...pass out."

"Really! Here I thought you were invincible, but it turns out you are human."

"And now you know my Achilles heel."

"And you know mine."

The waiter comes over, and I realize we haven't so much as picked up our menus and have to ask her to come back. Once we order and she brings our salads, Bex stabs a forkful of hers and asks, "How is the launch of Nudge Out going?"

"Even better than we had hoped for. The reviews are coming in quite positive, as well. Everly thinks it has a lot to do with your interview, so thank you."

"Since this is the first week of the Eddie Award judging period, I've been slammed with work and haven't had time to even go in and look at the comments. But Nikki assures me that people love you. So thank *you*. It's been helping me out a lot, too."

Everly has told me that, too. That her viewers are loving both me and the product. I went to the comments myself yesterday, and there's a lot more to them than just that. There are haters, of course, but that's to be expected of anything. There are also enough people who are "shipping" us as a couple that it's making me uncomfortable.

I might have enjoyed being on camera and talking about my company and our products, and I might have agreed that sharing a few tidbits about myself was important. And it might boost my ego a bit knowing that Bex is drawn to me enough that other people can see it too. But so many commenters are discussing our relationship. Some are guessing at what point our relationship currently is at. Others are predicting where it might go. Some of them even fast-forward to marriage and kids. It's all too much.

Luckily, all that is stuff that my family and the people in my social circles aren't likely to see. All the memes that are going viral are another story, and each one feels like a potential ticking time bomb that's going to blow up on me.

What am I doing?

"So, we're filming our final interview tomorrow," Bex says as she pulls out her phone and gives it a little shake. "Are you ready to see what Nudge Out suggests we do?"

I nod. Honestly, I'm a little worried about what it will suggest. But Bex hadn't given me any notice on what the last two activities were going to be before I showed up to film, so at least with this one, I'll get a heads-up.

Her face lights up as she opens the app. She places the phone on the table between us and meets my eyes, a smile on her face. "Are you ready?"

I nod. "Tap it."

Bex touches the Nudge Me Out button, and the suggestion comes up on the screen. She reads it out loud. "'Are you ready to be nudged out of your comfort zone? Several factors were taken into consideration for this suggestion. Career factors: creative pursuits. Profile factors: a high tolerance for change. Location factors…' And then it lists a bunch of places I've gone since you installed the app on my phone that it saw as relevant."

She scrolls down.

"'Nudge Out suggests you should try… a painting class!' Wow. I hadn't even thought of that. Oh, and look—it brought up painting classes near me that I can sign up for. I am impressed. Very clever. I hope you're up for a painting class, because there's one tomorrow night at eight, and I'm signing us up right now."

That answers my question of what I'm doing and where. Plus, I'm spending time with a woman who is brave, daring, decisive, unpredictable, and who will stand her ground. She also just happens to be beautiful. "Let's do it."

She's putting in our information when I see from my periphery someone coming to our table. I assume it's our waitress or someone from the kitchen bringing the main course, but no—it's a tall, rather good-looking man who is clearly not an employee.

"Well, if it isn't Bex Sterling."

Bex looks up, flinching in surprise. "Derek."

He grabs an empty chair from the table beside us, swings it to where the back of the chair is against the table, and then sits down, resting his folded arms on the back of the chair. "I saw you sitting over here and thought I'd come by to say hi."

Bex looks at him, confusion on her face, but manages to pull her eyes off him and look back to me. "Roman, this is Derek Baylor. He and I went out a few times. Derek, this is my date, Roman Powell."

Derek holds out a hand and I shake it, wishing I could instead just give the guy a friendly shove back to his own table. "Nice to meet you, mate," the guy says. "I like wearing wild socks, too. It looks like our girl, here, has a type." Then he winks.

I really don't like the guy calling Bex "our girl," and I don't like that wink. Or the fact that he's read the *Business Success* article. I don't like the guy at all and wish he'd just walk away already.

"It's good seeing you again, Bex. We need to catch up." And then the guy just sits there, like he wants us to catch up right now.

I pull at my collar, wishing a cool breeze would find its way through the restaurant and help me out. I'm just opening my mouth to tell the guy to get lost, but Bex beats me to it.

"Sure. Some other time. You'll have to excuse me right now, though. I need to get back to my date."

"Right, right. I wouldn't want to interrupt. Bex," he nods his head at her. "Roman." Another nod. "Enjoy your meal." And then he saunters back to his table.

"Well, if that wasn't strange, I don't know what was," Bex says. "I swear that wasn't even his real personality." She glances back in the direction the guy walked and then shakes her head. "Where were we? Oh yeah." She picks up her phone and taps a few things. "Okay, we are all set for tomorrow at eight. It's about fifteen minutes from here, just inside Portland—not too far from your work, actually. I could meet you at your offices and we could drive to it together. Do you want to grab a quick bite to eat from a deli or something before we go to the class?"

I love this take-charge side of her. How am I going to say no to that?

Our waitress brings our food a moment later and we start eating. About halfway through our meal, someone else walks up to our table.

"Hello, Bex."

Bex nearly chokes on the bite of cod she just took when she looks up. "Justin! Hi. What are you doing here?"

He turns around the chair that the last guy vacated and sits down. "Just visiting my sister. How have you been?"

"I'm good. Roman, Justin Tyler. Justin, Roman Powell. We have also gone on a few dates."

Either this is the strangest coincidence I've ever encountered, or Bex just dates a lot of people in Gresham. I smile and shake the guy's hand to be polite. As soon as the guy leaves, I'll have to ask the waitress if she'll take the extra chair far, far away, so no one else will get any bright ideas.

"My sister just had a baby. Jana—do you remember her? I think the two of you met that time we went to the concert in the park. Anyway, her baby is the cutest thing."

Justin pulls out his phone to show Bex pictures, and I hold in a growl. Can he not see that we're in the middle of a date? Bex glances in my direction and mouths *Sorry* as Justin shows his phone to her.

"Oh, she is adorable."

Then a guy walks up to the other side of the table, and before Bex even turns her attention to him, he grabs an empty chair from a table on that side and sits down. Bex hasn't looked over yet, so he holds out his hand to me. "Hi. My name's Darshan. I've gone on a couple of dates with Bex—thought I'd pop over and say hi."

"Roman," I say as I shake the guy's hand.

Bex looks over, baffled that Darshan is sitting at our table now. "Hi, Darshan. Wow, it's been a while. How are you?"

"I'm good! Living the dream. You're looking fantastic. I catch your show now and then—you're getting more and more popular all the time."

You'd think that Justin would leave when someone else pulls a seat up to the table, but he stays. Of course, having me here hasn't kept him away, so maybe I shouldn't have expected anything different.

Someone from the other side of the restaurant walks over, bringing a chair with him. He plunks it down right between Justin and Bex and takes a seat. "Mind if I join this party?"

Bex closes her eyes a small moment like she's hoping that when she opens them, all this craziness will be gone. It's what I'm wishing for, too. "Roman, everyone, this is Enzo Parks."

Justin holds out a hand. "Past flame of Bex's?"

The guy nods. "Went on three dates. You, too?" After

Justin nods back, Enzo looks around the table. "What are we celebrating?"

"A first date between Bex and me," I say, hoping they all get the hint.

They don't. Enzo even flags down the waitress and orders a drink. I just happen to glance over at the hostess's table, where the hostess is looking at our table while a man points at it, and then waves at me. As smooth as can be, the man grabs an extra chair at a table along the way, then sets it down right between me and Darshan. "Hi," he says, tipping his head at me. "I'm Carlos. I used to date Bex."

"Roman. I'm currently dating Bex. As in right this moment."

The guy nods, and we both look at Bex, who hasn't even seemed to notice that Carlos has joined the table because she's talking to a guy who just grabbed the waitress's attention and asked for a chair. Then he asks Bex to scoot over to make room.

"Roman, this is Vaughan. Oh. Carlos. I didn't see you come in." She looks baffled at the seven people now crowding around our table for two. "You all just happened to be here eating at the same time I am here on a date?"

"Saul!"

I turn around to see who Bex's attention got pulled to, just as another man grabs a chair and carries it to our table, squeezing in between me and Justin. He says hello to Bex, then starts introducing himself to everyone else around the table, and each of them tells him their names. If all these guys want the table, they can have it. They can have the rest of the food, too. I just need to free Bex from her adoring ghosts of dates past and go find somewhere quiet to finish our date.

"Stop!" Bex says. "Okay, someone tell me what's going on here. This was definitely not a coincidence."

Everyone is silent for a few moments, and then Justin leans forward. "Check your X notifications."

She pulls out her phone and taps a few things. Her eyes scan the screen for a moment, and then her hand flies to her mouth. She turns to glance at all the people in the restaurant at the other tables, who all seem to be getting a kick out of watching this go down. Several even have phones out, video recording or taking pictures. Then she looks at me.

"Apparently someone—I don't recognize the name—saw Derek come over. The guy recognized us and posted about it."

"What did he say?"

She hesitates a moment before she passes me the phone, and I read the post.

At dinner w/gf & see @TheRealBexSterling eating with #Nudge-Out's Roman Powell. Her old bf pulls up a chair & the look on Roman's face is priceless! Please, X, send anyone Bex has dated to #Kitchen712 to do the same. Repost & tag or text anyone you know. I'll update w/results.

I scroll through the thread—the guy has posted a picture every time a new guy shows up, complete with some commentary on how I react. I look in the direction the guy must've been seated to get the pictures he did and see a man in his upper twenties sitting in a booth across from a woman

I can only assume is his girlfriend. The man salutes me. I chuckle and give the guy a nod back. Not to thank him in any way. More as an acknowledgment of a game well-played.

"Well, guys," Darshan says, standing up, "I think that's our cue to leave. Bex, it truly was good to see you again."

Everyone else follows Darshan's lead and stands as well, returning their chairs from where they got them. Another guy walks up and says, "Aww, am I too late? Did I miss the party?"

"Hi, Jack," Bex says. "And yes, you did."

"Bummer. Hey, anyone want to join me at the bar, since we're already here?"

About half the guys stay and join Jack at the bar, but at least they aren't around our table anymore. Bex still looks a bit flustered, though.

"What do you say we get dessert to go and get out of here?" I ask.

Bex smiles. "That sounds perfect. I'd love that."

Thirty minutes later, we are wrapped in a blanket I had in my trunk and sitting on a bench at my favorite place in the city—in the Tsuru Island part of Main City Park. Beautiful plants and pathways surround us, a creek is close by enough that we can hear its gurgling, the sky is clear so we can actually see the stars, and Bex is snuggled against me.

"You need to try one of the pears with the sauce," Bex says, holding her spoon out to me.

I eat the bite and am surprised at how great it tastes. I've never been a huge fan of pears, so I've never ordered the dessert before. It's good enough that I'll have to order it for myself next time.

"Okay, then you have to try a bite of mine." I get a forkful of my volcano cake, making sure to get some of the molten lava center and feed it to her. I smile when she closes her eyes in blissful contentment. This is definitely better than staying at the restaurant.

She sets her dessert on the bench beside her. "I had fun tonight."

"Even with the craziness?"

"Especially with the craziness."

I set my dessert aside and raise an eyebrow.

"I liked seeing you ruffled." She snuggles back into me. "You handled it well."

I like that she hasn't taken responsibility for them all showing up or felt like she needed to apologize for it happening since she had no control over it. She just sees it as a mutual issue to tackle together. It's refreshing.

Bex sits up straight and turns to me. "The Eddie Awards are coming up."

I brush a lock of hair back from her temple with my fingertips so I can see her beautiful eyes better. "And you are going to knock them dead."

"No, I'm talking about the ceremony itself, where they present the awards. It's in a different major city every year, and this year it's in Portland, so it isn't even far. Will you go with me? I probably won't win, but it'll be fun to get dressed up all fancy for it."

I was excited to be able to spend time with Bex tonight

without cameras, but it seems like they follow her wherever she goes. I hate that people took pictures of our date and posted about it. So, the thought of a date where people will be taking pictures not so surreptitiously doesn't sound appealing at all. If it was anyone other than Bex, I would tell them no. But this is Bex. And I care about this award because she cares about it.

"I would love to go with you."

She smiles at me—a smile so brilliant that the stars above can't compete. Then she kisses me, and all my worries about our date becoming public knowledge fade away.

CHAPTER 15

Bex

I'VE BEEN SEEING Roman enough lately that I worry if I'm not careful, he's going to turn into a habit. Like my habit of starting each morning off with one square of fine dark chocolate. It's something I look forward to. Savor. And feel like the day just isn't right when I don't have it.

"Hi," I breathe as he gets into my car. I've dated plenty of guys who wear cologne. Some good-smelling and some not-so-good-smelling. Some wear just a hint, while others seem to take a shower in it. I've also dated plenty of guys who don't wear cologne. Actually, it's not something I normally notice unless it's a bad smell, or one that's too strong, or one that just really doesn't fit the guy.

But when Roman steps into the car, the scent of him comes in with him, and it's glorious. It doesn't even smell like cologne, exactly. It's more like it's just a part of him—a scent that is clean and fresh. Maybe birch? Bergamot? I don't know. Maybe it is cologne, and the guy is just ten levels beyond pro at picking out the right scent. I hope it stays in my car forever and ever. Then, whenever I need a pick-me-up and I can't be around Roman, I can just go sit in my car and breathe in the scent of him.

Wow, I am falling ridiculously hard for him.

"No Enoch today?"

I shake my head as I pull out into traffic. "He has a basketball tournament, and Nikki is at a weekend getaway. I have another backup videographer I sometimes use, but I thought this one could be easily filmed by my friend Tripod there in the back seat. Plus, I figured it might be a little less intimidating to everyone else in the class if there wasn't someone videoing it."

I looked up the address of the painting class earlier in the day. It's in a pedestrian mall with cute shops and plenty of places to eat, and the drive isn't long. Once I get parked, we find the shop where the painting class will be, then head two shops down to a cute little café with outdoor seating.

As soon as we finish ordering, a teenage girl walks up to us, doing a pretty good job of not acting nervous except for the way she fiddles with the keys in her hand. "You're Bex Sterling, aren't you?"

"I am. What's your name?"

"Lanie. I can't believe I'm actually meeting you. I love your show, and I want to start my own someday. I've been watching yours for like two years, obsessing over every-thing. Can I ask you for some advice about running a business?"

I'm pretty sure I hear Roman make a faint scoffing sound that he tries to hide. I ignore him and say to the girl, "Sure!"

"I start college in the fall, and I was thinking of doing a marketing major and entrepreneurship minor. Do you think that's good? Or would a different major be better? And should I wait until I'm all done with school and have everything ready to start? Or is it better to start now so I can get practice, and just build slowly?"

I answer her questions until the woman behind the counter says, "Excuse me—your order is ready."

The girl thanks me profusely and goes back to join her friends, while Roman and I take our tray outside and find an open table. As Roman takes our sandwiches off the tray and places one in front of each of us, I say, "Did I hear you scoff when she asked for business advice?"

"I just thought it was a strange question because it's not really a business." He hands us each a drink.

"I have a business license and incorporation papers that say otherwise. But I'm curious to know why you think it isn't."

He looks sheepish, like he knows he's in trouble. "I guess it was just because your only employees are your sister and your nephew."

"For a long time, it was just me. And it was still every bit as much of a business as it is now. We both make digital products, Roman. The only difference is that my business gets paid by companies showing ads and yours does by people buying apps." It bothers me that he doesn't seem to have the same respect for my business that he has for his own.

He rubs his hands over his face. "You're right. I apologize —that was very rude of me. Let me make it up to you."

"Ooo. I like the sound of that. Will it involve kissing?"

A smile lifts the corners of his mouth. "There can definitely be kissing. And how about I surprise you at the inn some random evening by showing up with dessert?"

"If it can be pie, then you're on."

In between taking bites of our sandwiches, I tell him a little more about what to expect tonight. We've been working on such short notice, not only to give the Nudge Out app time to collect enough data about me but also because all of the interviews with Roman have been in addition to my normal production schedule.

"I called the owner of the shop where we'll have the painting class. There are eight people registered, so we won't be able to interview while the class is going on. But she said that if we can get there a few minutes early, we can film an introduction before it starts, and then film the rest of the interview at the end."

"That sounds great."

The weather is beautiful, and I wish I could just hang out at the diner, chatting and watching the cars and pedestrians go by for hours while I sit close to Roman, leaning my head on his shoulder. But this interview isn't going to film itself.

So the moment we finish, we stand up, collect our trash, and head toward the garbage receptacle. As I'm dumping the tray, the lid of the garbage can catches on the tray, causing me to dump all the crumbs from our sandwiches down my front. I'm just brushing it off and checking to make sure no sauce has jumped ship and is catching a ride on my shirt right before filming when I notice Roman stiffen beside me.

"Dad."

His tone is full of surprise and guilt, like a kid getting caught watching TV when he's supposed to be doing homework. I look up to see a man who, by the strong shoulders and jawline, is very much Roman's dad. The resemblance between the two is uncanny. Except his dad has gray in his sideburns, wrinkles around his eyes, and the aged skin of someone twenty-five or thirty years older, and has clearly spent a much larger percentage of his life not being in touch with his more calm, peaceful side. He is dressed in a suit, and so are the two men and one woman with him.

"Roman! What a surprise to see you here. What brings you to Portland? And with this lovely young lady?"

I stop brushing the crumbs off my blouse and jeans and hope I haven't missed any.

"Dad, this is Bex Sterling." Roman pauses a long moment, like he isn't quite sure what to introduce me as, then goes with, "She is a targeting specialist that we are using to make sure we are reaching the right audience. We just had a dinner meeting to go over some things. Bex, this is my dad, Doctor Richmond Powell the fourth."

"Nice to meet you, Bex Sterling." He reaches out and shakes my hand, then motions to the people standing with him on the sidewalk. "And these are some of my board members—we were just meeting to discuss strategy, as well. Are you an employee of Roman's, or are you freelance?"

I eye Roman. "Freelance."

"Well, then, I might have to see about having you do some work at our company as well. Now if you'll excuse us, we've got a reservation at Grill House." He motions at a restaurant three buildings down, gives us a nod, and then the four of them keep walking while Roman and I head to my car to get my tripod and video camera.

As soon as his dad is out of earshot, I stop next to my car, hands on my hips. "Why didn't you tell him my real job? Or what we were here doing?"

He stops too, turning to me as he lets out a big breath. "Because my dad isn't a nice person. And it's none of his business."

"He seemed nice enough. Are you saying he would've been rude if he knew that I'm a YouTuber?"

"It's more complicated than that."

I look out at nothing in the distance, feeling ruffled about the conversation. I don't know much about his dad at all, and I recognize that there's a lot of history and father/son dynamics between the two that I don't know about yet. But after his scoff when the teenager asked about my business earlier, his hesitation when talking about me to his dad bothers me and makes me feel like Roman doesn't respect my job very much. I look back at him. "Does he know that we've been shooting these interviews?"

"No. And hopefully, he never will. Like I said, he's not a nice guy."

I start walking toward the shop again, arms crossed. I'm not upset because he wants to protect me. It's that it doesn't seem like it's mostly about him protecting me. It seemed more like he'd been embarrassed to tell his dad the truth about me—about my job and about the fact that we aren't here for an audience-targeting meeting.

I need to know how he feels. From the start, I have been

worried that he isn't the right guy for me. And then, because of all the ways in which he *is* perfect, I've let down my defenses. But I can't start a relationship with a guy who doesn't value me or my chosen career. So, if those defenses need to go back up, I want to know now—not later, when I'm even more invested. I don't want to experience what happened to my sister.

"Roman, do you respect me, as a YouTuber?"

He stops walking and the look on his face is softer. "I do, Bex. I think you are amazing at it, and I can see why you have so many subscribers and fans everywhere we go. I didn't mean to come off sounding like I didn't." I search his eyes and see truth there. Then he reaches out and pulls me close, like he doesn't care who sees, and kisses my temple.

"Thank you. But…camera…in my ribs."

"Oh!" Roman pulls back, and I adjust the camera strap so it rests in a more comfortable spot.

When we arrive at the shop, I set up my equipment right between our two easels, so our faces will be in frame. Then I shake out my arms and try to clear my head of leftover annoyance before I start to film. Not everyone has a great relationship with their parents. That's all it was.

Both Roman and I put on aprons with the *Paint Date* logos on them and sit down at the spots where we will be painting. Before starting the camera, I look over at Roman, and he gives me that smile that melts my insides, his eyes scanning my face like he really loves what he sees there.

I turn on the camera with my remote and start filming the introduction. I take out my phone and show them what the app suggested when I tapped *Nudge Me Out*, and how it even found a place near me with openings.

"So here we are," Roman says, holding up a paintbrush, "ready to paint. Even though I've never done this before in my life."

"What about art class in school when you were a kid? You never painted then?"

"No, I did. I just didn't paint actual things. Here, we are painting"—he glances at the front where the painting we will be duplicating is placed—"a starry night sky with a couple kissing in front of a full moon.

"I knew how awful my drawing skills were, so in school, instead of painting whatever we were supposed to paint, I just painted 'abstract art.' I found that if I could tell my teachers a good story about the meaning behind the painting or about the choices I made, they always accepted it. I was either really good at convincing them that I knew what I was doing, or they just knew that there was no help for me and were glad I was at least picking up the brush. Based on the art history classes I took later on, where we discussed actual abstract art, I think it was the latter."

I laugh, shaking my head. I'm grateful that he is willing to share personal things in our interviews now, and I'm impressed that he does it without much prodding at all. He is giving me exactly what I need for this interview, just like he has for the three others. And he is still here doing them with me—he didn't quit after the first one like I worried he would. He must trust that my final edited video will be something he's proud of. Surely that means that he respects my job and that the incidents today were just a fluke.

Right?

"How about you?" he asks. "Is this new for you?"

"Not completely new, but it has been a good long while since I last picked up a brush."

We chat for a minute about the Nudge Out app and the things it is doing for people who have been using it. Roman even tells a few stories of people who have contacted them to let them know the new things they have tried and how it has boosted their confidence in doing hard things.

People who are taking the class with us start trickling in, so I stop the recording and move the tripod behind us so viewers can see our paintings as we work and see the instructor as she teaches. It will all be edited down to just the highlights.

Roman rolls his shoulders. He sits on the stool that is placed in front of his easel, one foot resting on the bottom rung, his knee bouncing.

"Oh my goodness, you're nervous."

"About having your viewers see what I'm painting? No. What gave you that idea?" Roman keeps his eyes on the painting at the front.

A smile plays on my lips. Normally, Roman shows only confidence, whether he has to fake it or not. Seeing this anxious side of him is endearing. Maybe because he is actually letting me see that side. It wasn't so long ago that he wouldn't have. "Getting nudged a little too far out of your comfort zone, huh?"

He turns on his stool so he is facing me and leans forward before whispering, "What do you say we keep that our little secret?" And then he kisses me. It's a lingering peck on the lips, but it's enough to make me feel lightheaded.

That bouncing of his knee, though, continues to tell me how nervous he is. This interview isn't going to go well if the guy I'm interviewing is so distracted by his thoughts of messing up something he isn't familiar with.

"What about the painting are you least looking forward to?"

He nods toward the front. "The people."

I look at the painting at the front that we will be recreating. The focal point is definitely the moon. In front of it is a woman and a man facing each other, both standing with their hands behind their backs and bent at the waist, leaning forward to kiss. "Even though they're just silhouettes and not very big?"

He nods. "I paint abstract art when drawing is involved, remember?"

"How about this." I push our easels a little closer together and turn my canvas so it is taller up and down instead of sideways, then do the same for Roman's. "We'll each paint half. Since the couple is right in the middle, you'll only have to paint the girl, and I'll paint the guy."

"Okay. But my girl is going to look like a stick figure still. I hope you're okay with that."

The instructor has given us each a big circle that's sticky, like tape, and she demonstrates by putting the circle in the middle of her canvas where the moon will be. Then she puts paint right onto the canvas—black in the top corners, then purple, then a deep blue, then a lighter blue. She shows how to first spread the paint and blend the colors slightly, and then use a stippling brush to make the paint look like the night sky.

Roman and I start by trying to each put our half of the moon in the right place on our canvases and have it line up correctly so it'll still look like an actual circle. As we struggle, the instructor comes around to see how everyone is doing. When she sees we are each doing half, she pushes our easels together so that our canvases are touching. "You must have them touching if you want them to look right."

If this were a date, I'd be all for that. But this is an interview where I am interviewing the CEO of a company, not interviewing a date for my viewers to weigh in on. Not that the interview is supposed to be stuffy and professional—I want it to be fun. I'll just have to work extra hard to not show how attracted I am to the man.

The painting is going pretty well. The night sky is kind of like abstract art, so Roman actually appears to be enjoying himself. And so am I. We're both working on getting the top middle part to look right, and we are only a few inches apart. "You smell so amazing," I breathe. Then I suck in a breath and look back at the camera. "Nikki's going to have to edit that out."

A smile tugs at his lips, and then he closes the last couple of inches between us and gives me a peck on the lips. "While she's at it, she should probably edit that out, too."

I look at this man's beautiful face before I go back to work. I love the feeling of both of us being side by side, working together on the same project, helping each other to figure out what parts need to change and what parts are perfect like they are. This painting is definitely turning out a lot better with both of us working together than it would be if either of us were working apart.

And there are definitely a lot of parts Nikki is going to have to edit out so I don't totally give away how I feel about this man.

Our instructor has us remove the tape circle, revealing the huge, white moon in the night sky. Seriously, we could be done right now and I would call our painting a job well done. But apparently, the moon has to be painted, and the instructor shows us how to make it look like the moon. Then we paint black along the bottom for the ground, with little blades of grass coming up from it.

I am painting the grass at the edge near Roman's. I move my brush back to get more paint right as he leans in to paint the fine blades, and my paintbrush goes right across his cheek.

He turns to me, a giant black streak on his cheek, like a cat's whisker, and I gasp. "I am so sorry."

He doesn't say a word—he just reaches out and paints what I am pretty sure looks like a cat's nose on my nose. Then he goes back to work like nothing has happened.

I turn to the camera. "I guess that evens the score."

We watch as the instructor shows us how to paint the silhouettes of the couple about to kiss.

"Well," I say, "remember how the part of painting that you hated most as a kid was drawing the picture on it before painting? You don't have to draw on this one."

"I'm not sure 'can't draw it first' is any better than 'can't draw at all.'" He motions at the instructor. "How did she even know where to use the black paint to make it look like a person without drawing it first?"

I study our beautiful moon and night sky. "Maybe we should paint something other than people, then."

Forty-five minutes later, after finishing our paintings, using the handheld fans to dry them, and filming the end of our interview, we walk out to my car with our masterpieces.

Roman holds his up in the glow of the streetlight and studies it. "I can't believe you had us paint two cats instead of two people."

"Oh, come on. You know it was easier than painting a person."

"I painted a black avocado."

"But a black avocado with cat ears and a tail, so it counts as a cat."

I smile as he carefully places his painting in the back seat of my car. He might not admit it out loud, but he is proud of it. Just like I wouldn't admit out loud that even though this is an interview and not a date, I have still enjoyed myself more than I have on any date I've gone on with anyone else.

CHAPTER 16

Roman

I WALK OUT of my office building and immediately call Bex. Sometime over the past several weeks, calling Bex first whenever I have something I want to share has just become what I do.

"Well?" she asks, forgoing a hello, eager anticipation coloring the single word.

"They signed on the dotted line. It's official."

Her excited shout is loud enough that I have to pull the phone away from my ear for a moment. "Roman! I'm so thrilled for you!"

Adrenaline is coursing through my body, and it makes me want to run and leap over things. Like a fence. My car. My office building. The investors said they wanted to invest in my company around the time that the third interview with Bex aired, but I held back my own celebrations until the paperwork was done and everything was official. Now, though. Now I am letting myself be fully thrilled.

"I couldn't have done it without you, Bex." I unlock my car, start it, and let the car's Bluetooth take over the call.

"I know." I can hear the smile in her voice through the car's speakers.

"And not just because of the interviews. Although that did make a big difference with them. But I couldn't have done it without you staying up to brainstorm with me and pushing me to try things with my business that I hadn't tried before. I owe you."

"You agreed to put on a monkey suit and spend hours at an awards gala with me on Saturday. I think that is enough to call us even."

As I pull onto the road and head toward Interstate 84 to make the thirty-minute drive to my parents', I chuckle softly. I am equal parts dreading the gala and excited about it. Bex assumes that the parts I am dreading are the suit and the small talk. But I like dressing nice, and I like talking to people.

I'm not about to correct her because then I'd have to tell her the real reason—that I'm worried about what my peers and my family will think if they know Bex and I are dating. Not because she isn't the most amazing person on the planet. But because I know that they think like I used to, so not only will they see her job as not being legit, but they'll see it as frivolous. Unimportant. I realize now how wrong I was in thinking that way. But they haven't had those same realizations, and they just happen to be an extremely judgmental group of people.

Not that they won't find out eventually, but I want to keep it our little secret for as long as possible. As long as I can see Bex often. I need her in my life like I need food, business projects, and sleep. Actually, I could do without sleep if it meant seeing her more often.

"Is it weird that I kind of miss filming the interviews?" I ask her.

I can almost hear that brilliant smile of hers through the phone as she says, "I think you just miss me."

"True. Are you sure I can't see you tomorrow?"

"Not unless you want to crash the female entrepreneur's social."

"And I've got this business reception at my parents' tonight."

"Saturday it is, then. But on the plus side, you'll get to tell your dad about the investors tonight. He's going to be pretty proud of you for that."

I smile just thinking about it.

———

I arrive at my parents' early enough that no guests have arrived yet, but not so early that they don't already have April, the college student they always hire whenever they host a function, on staff to answer the door.

As soon as I say hello to April, I hear the quick clacking of my mom's heels on the hardwood floor.

"Roman," she says, arms outstretched. I give her a hug, and then she pushes back on my shoulders to meet my eyes. "You're here early. Is something up?"

"I just wanted to share some news before everyone got here. Is Dad busy?"

"He's in his office."

We both walk down the hall and step through the doorway onto the plush carpet. My dad looks up at us from where he sits behind a mahogany desk, shelves full of books and business awards framing him.

"I had my final meeting with the investors today." I try to play it cool, but I can't stop the smile that forms on my face.

Dr. Richmond Powell IV, D.B.A. stands. "And?"

"We exceeded the requirements they had set forth by so much that they decided to invest fifty percent more than they had originally offered. We signed the papers less than an hour ago."

"That is fantastic news!" He comes around the table to shake my hand. Then, he actually pulls me into a hug—something that happens so infrequently I can't remember when the last time was. "Good work, son."

My mom gives me a hug and tells me congratulations as well, and then my dad motions to one of the padded chairs in front of the desk. "Sit, sit. I want to hear all about it."

Then my dad actually sits in the other chair instead of going around his desk to sit behind it. He never sits beside me like this—he always takes the spot where he has the advantage of more power. So I tell him all about the presentation I gave them last week, conveniently leaving out the part about how the investors wanted me to do more things like the interviews with Bex.

"I am so proud of you."

It feels amazing to hear my dad say those words after having gone so long since I last heard them.

My dad turns to my mom. "It looks like I have a river rafting trip to plan!"

Seeing the excitement on my dad's face is going to fuel me for a very long time. I'd been thinking I wouldn't ever be able to earn the trip, but I finally have.

More than a dozen of my peers are at the reception—mostly CEOs, business partners, and other business moguls my dad knows—and every single one of them has brought their significant other. Even my brother, Legend, who broke up with Briza a week and a half ago, has brought a woman he's dating. Not only do I feel very alone and miss Bex terribly, but I also feel very guilty about not having invited her. Especially since I knew she was free and wanted to see me.

But I am so worried that people will start asking questions and things won't go well. And I certainly don't want Bex to have to experience it.

Everyone is standing in clusters in my parents' back gardens and patio, drinks in hand, chatting with each other. I make a point to go from group to group, being friendly and chatting, so I never appear to be alone. It might help appearances, but it doesn't help my longing for a partner by my side.

I wasn't even aware of how much I wanted a partner until I started dating Bex. Before, I just thought I needed a date—and an eventual wife. I've dated plenty, but never anyone who I could see as a partner. Clearly, I've been dating the wrong people.

I pull out my phone when I hear the ding and see another email notification from Tarak about being on his social media panel. I really need to stop procrastinating the inevitable and tell the guy no.

I slide the phone back into my pocket and join in on a conversation with my brother, Drake, Drake's wife, Claire, Lucia, a friend who is the CEO of another app company, and her husband, along with one of my dad's board members and the guy's wife. When the conversation lulls, I say to Drake, "How did things go with that company you've been creating the business strategy for?"

"And…" Drake says, dragging out the word, "new topic! Let's talk about memes that have made you laugh lately. Did you all see the one with Roman and Bex Sterling from *Bexlandia* staring at the deer, and she leans over to him and says, 'I'm pretty sure people have been feeding this one.'"

I wince as everyone in our little group laughs. My brother was frustrated with that company the last time we talked, so I should've known not to ask. But throwing me under the bus to get the conversation off him is a low blow.

The sentence Drake had said by itself didn't warrant such a hearty laugh from everyone, which means they have all seen the meme. Great. I shoot my brother a look.

"My favorite, though," Lucia says, "was the one that read *The moment I learned Santa wasn't real,* above an animated gif of the blanket fort coming down on you two."

The six of them are laughing enough that it's drawing people from other little groups to join the conversation. I glance at my dad, who is deep in conversation over by the camellias. Good. I just need him to stay there.

"I liked the one with the mannequin," Lucia's husband, Mateo, says. "Did you guys see it? It was a still shot of

Roman looking at the mannequin like it was one of those stone angels from *Dr. Who* and it was going to attack him if he looked away. At the bottom, it said, *My reaction when my friend who just joined a multi-level marketing company says he wants to come over and chat.*"

Heat has been slowly building in my face and I'm sure it's to the point where it's visible to everyone.

"Have you seen the one with him smashing the pickleball?" someone asks from behind me. I don't even have a chance to turn to see who it is before my buddy, Shreedhar, says, "I liked the one even more that just loops his reaction when he aimed wrong and sent the ball right at Bex."

"How do you even have time to do interviews like that?" a fellow CEO, Archer, says. "My business keeps me so busy that I don't think I could ever pull that off."

I grind my teeth. Archer doesn't actually want to know the answer—it's an underhanded dig at the way I run my business, insinuating that I'm letting my CEO duties slip.

"I like the ones where people are shipping them as a couple," Legend's new girlfriend says. We haven't even been officially introduced yet, so I don't even know her name, nor had I noticed my brother join the crowd around me. "Like the one where someone Photoshopped them into a boat on Mirror Lake with a blanket as the sail."

Someone starts telling about one that has something to do with painting and cats, but I don't hear it because my dad has noticed that most of the people have gathered into one group and are laughing, so now he is on his way over. This cannot be good.

He is all smiles, but just under the surface, I can tell he

doesn't like not being in on whatever is happening. "It sounds like all the fun is over here."

Several people nod, all while a chorus of "Did you see the one where…" continues around us.

"What am I missing?"

One of the guys my dad golfs with claps Richmond on the shoulder. "Didn't you know? Your boy here is an internet sensation!"

I wish they would all stop. Or better yet, that they would've never started. I wish that my dream of none of them ever seeing a single thing about my interviews had come true. I wish for a lot of things, including the ability to teleport so I could get myself out of here instantly.

Instead, everyone fills in my dad, and with as much as everyone is laughing, you'd think this is a college frat party instead of a respectable business reception.

"Richmond," Mom says, "could I get you to help me bring out some more refreshments for our guests?"

Dad nods, and then he leans close to me. "As soon as you can slip away, I want to talk to you in my office."

Then he heads into the house. Not to help bring out refreshments—they've hired servers for the evening. Mom has probably noticed the look on his face that says he's about to make a scene in front of everyone, so she's getting him away from the crowd. I give him seven minutes to cool down, knowing that's about the length of his patience before he starts fuming that I haven't come in.

When I walk in through the patio door, Mom gives my shoulders a quick squeeze. "Good luck, honey." Then she slips back outside to our guests.

When I enter Dad's office, he's sitting behind the desk. No more sitting side by side—this time, he wants to intimidate. And great—he's looking at his laptop. I don't even need to guess what he's been watching.

Why do I feel like a kid again, about to get into trouble for bad grades or for toilet-papering the boys' restroom that one time in third grade?

Dad just keeps looking at whatever he's watching for several excruciatingly long minutes, not even acknowledging that I've walked into the room. Eventually, he pushes the laptop aside. Which, honestly, isn't any better, because now his eyes are piercing into me. And he still isn't talking—just studying me. He has always been the master at getting the upper hand and making anyone else in the room feel like an ant. A little tiny ant who just spilled milk on the floor.

Finally, he speaks. "I thought you had learned a hard lesson with that *Business Success* interview. But then you went and made a fool of yourself on a stage with two million viewers. A stage that can be accessed anywhere in the world, no less. And that's not even counting the number of people who saw the memes once they went viral. I can't say I've ever been more disappointed in you."

He wants me to respond. But I have no idea what kind of response he could possibly want. So I go for the truth, to see how that goes. "Those investors who just gave LivenUP a pile of money? They liked the *Business Success* interview. They said they would only invest if they could see more of that. Of me showing the spark that told them LivenUP was going places and that I was going to lead them there. Those interviews I did showed them that. That was why they invested."

Dad pounds his fist on the desk, making everything on it —and my heart—jump. "You carry the Powell name, Roman! That means something. People hear that name and they know they are going to get someone who is a professional through and through. That name is a gift, and you need to treat it as such."

He clenches his jaw, giving me a look of disgust that he has perfected over the years. "Instead, you're trying to bring down the family. You don't change who you are just because a group of investors wants to give you a pile of money to do so."

All I can think of is how I haven't changed who I am— I've let the real me come forward in those interviews. *That* was a gift. One I hadn't been expecting that Bex had given to me.

Dad turns his attention back to the laptop, clicking a few things. Then he turns back to me. "That audience targeting specialist I saw you with a few weeks ago—that was her, wasn't it? She's the woman behind all of this."

"She is the producer of *Bexlandia*, yes." I ignore the flinch on his face when I mention *Bexlandia*. "She wasn't 'behind' it —we went to her to ask for the interview when my head of social media and marketing identified her audience as our target audience for Nudge Out."

"Then you need to fire your head of social media and marketing and do what you need to do to get those interviews taken down."

Yeah, like I'm going to do either of those things.

He studies me for an uncomfortably long moment. "You're dating this woman." It's a statement, not a question, but it's clear he doesn't know the answer. He's fishing. But I'm done hiding our relationship.

"Yes."

Richmond lets out a long, slow breath. "Is it a fling?"

"No."

"Roman, I don't think I need to remind you about the kind of woman you are expected to marry. She needs to be respectable and have a respectable career—not name her company something like *Bexlandia* and post simpleton content to a simpleton site. She needs to be someone who will respect the Powell name and the kind of public image we need to maintain."

"Dad, I—"

Richmond stands up. "I don't want to hear it, son." He walks to the door but pauses before he steps out. "Oh, and the Columbia River trip is off. You can see yourself out."

CHAPTER 17

Bex

"Oh my exclamation points, I can't believe how beautiful you look!" Peyton says. She is working on my hair for the awards ceremony, and my sister, Nikki, is putting the finishing touches on my makeup while I sit at the vanity in my bedroom.

Nikki nods. "I hope you win. But, girl, you are going to leave a trail of scorch marks all the way up to the stage if you do."

I look down at my silky, red, form-fitting, full-length dress. It isn't too low in the front, but the back does dip down quite a bit. "Do you think it's too much?"

"I think it's exactly enough," Nikki says. "Your entire female audience is going to be going insane experiencing this vicariously through you—living the dream, getting dressed up all fancy, looking incredible, and having everyone talking about how awesome the thing you created is. I know I am."

"Yep," Peyton says as she twists one of my curls to lay just right. "Especially since they know you well enough to know how down-to-earth you really are. I mean, they've been with you at the drugstore as you were getting Tylenol and socks. Your viewers know you are practically them."

I laugh. The drugstore thing wasn't some calculated move or part of some bigger-picture video I was posting. I had just remembered I needed to tell them about an event coming up where viewers could join me, and I happened to be in the drugstore when I remembered, so that's where I did the Facebook live video. "That's me. Tylenol and sock girl. Oh, hey, speaking of drugstores, guess who I saw when I was in Hillsboro on Monday? Brant. He looked awful, in case you were wondering."

Peyton looks at Nikki. "Is that your ex-husband?"

"The one and only."

"Oh," Peyton says. "I bet he looked awful. He lost you, after all."

Nikki just shakes her head as she awkwardly leans around Peyton to brush some bronzing powder on me while trying not to let her pregnant belly get in the way. "Stop. You all don't have to say that anymore. I am married to Dylan now, so what Brant looks like is completely irrelevant. I don't need his life to be awful for mine to be amazing."

I hold perfectly still while they work on me. "Although it probably is awful because the guy is a jerk. I'm so glad you found Dylan."

"Me, too. I just wish I hadn't thrown away all those years dating Brant and being engaged and married to him. I should've listened to you all when you warned me that he was a jerk or paid more attention to the warning signs. I wasted a lot of my life on him."

Is that what I'm doing with Roman? I had been convinced that he was a jerk from the beginning and had told myself to stay away. But then he thoroughly swept me off my feet. Am I being just like Nikki had been back when she was dating Brant and ignoring all the warning signs?

Well, I haven't been ignoring them, exactly. I've been calling him on them. Like when he'd scoffed when the girl had asked for business advice. Then I ignored them. Kind of like how I've ignored how distant and clipped his responses have been ever since he called to say the deal with the investors had been finalized a couple of days ago.

"Stand up, sis. Let's take a look at you."

I look in my full-length mirror. This dress really is incredible, and I still can't believe I found it. Especially because the red is the perfect tone for my skin color. Peyton has worked miracles with my hair—it has big chunky curls pulled up beautifully, making my neck look pretty awesome if I do say so myself.

And my makeup makes me look like I'm practically glowing. Not in a shiny "use me as a beacon to guide in lost ships" way. In an "I have so much awesome inside me, it's bursting out the only way it knows how—by making my skin glow" way. Which I will take any day of the week.

"You two are miracle workers, and I am so lucky to have you!"

Peyton squeals. "Oh, my stars and stripes, you are so pretty! Let's go show you to Addison and Ian and Timini!"

Nikki and Peyton run out of the room and race down the

stairs to get the others, so by the time I make it to the top of the stairs, all five of them are standing in a half-circle at the bottom, looking up at me.

I'm wearing four-inch heels, so I walk down the stairs a little slower than normal. With how dressed up I am and descending at this speed, I feel like it's either prom or a debutante thing, not just a prestigious web show award thing.

They all start *ooh*-ing and *ahh*-ing, so I stop for a dramatic pose. Timini snaps a picture on her phone.

"Okay, stop, guys. This is weird." I make it the rest of the way down the stairs.

"Seriously, Bex," Addison says, "you look absolutely beautiful."

Timini nods. "Stunning."

"You look ready to go on stage and win an award," Ian says.

"I still think you should've gotten a limo to drive you there." Peyton goes to the window by the door and moves the curtain aside. She claps her hands. "Oh, he's here!"

I turn to face the door as Peyton opens it wide. Roman had just been lifting his arm to knock and freezes when he sees me. Which seems appropriate, since I'm doing the same. He just looks so amazing in his suit! It's perfectly fitted and shows off those strong shoulders and arms, and his trim physique. He is one very beautiful man. I'm not going to be able to take my eyes off him all night.

I take a few steps toward him.

"Wow," he breathes. "You look incredible."

I come one step closer, to where we are only inches apart. "Right back atcha."

"You made my heart skip a beat."

I smile as I put my arms around his neck. "That sounds dangerous. You should probably get that looked into."

"Oh, I did. And I have a diagnosis."

"Yeah?"

He wisely bypasses my lipstick and places a soft kiss on my neck, right next to my ear, and whispers, "That I am very lucky to be on your arm tonight."

"Alright, alright, go already," Nikki says.

"Break a leg!" Peyton yells. "Do you say 'break a leg' for this? Probably not, because you have to climb stairs to get on the awards stage. Um…go win and don't trip!"

I laugh. "Thanks, Pey."

We walk out of the inn to the sounds of everyone wishing me luck. Roman opens my car door for me and once I'm seated, he makes sure the end of my dress is all inside before he shuts my door and goes around to his side to get in.

On the way to Portland, we talk about random things, but something is off with Roman. Instead of our chatting being easy, like it usually is, his answers are short, and my back hurts from carrying the conversation. So I eventually stop trying. Because, truthfully, I'm feeling a bit off, too. I've had a nagging feeling for weeks that I'm making a mistake by dating Roman. Until now, I've been ignoring it. But since Nikki put it into words, I can't stop thinking that there might be warning signs I'm ignoring.

Once we pull onto Morrison Bridge and cross the Willamette River, though, the excitement for the evening really starts to build. We go around the loop and onto Pacific Highway, and moments later, we're pulling up to the Portland Marriott Downtown Waterfront hotel.

We follow the signs posted for the Eddie Awards to a valet who is waiting to take the car. Roman once again opens my door, then holds my hand and helps me out. I've never been to the awards ceremony before, but I've always pored over the pictures, imagining what it would be like to be here.

My imagination hadn't quite captured what it would actually feel like. So, although I know there will be a red carpet lined with photographers, it feels so surreal to walk down it, hand-in-hand with Roman. My goal with *Bexlandia* hasn't ever been to win an Eddie—it's always been to connect with my audience authentically and to encourage them to seek out the awesome in their own lives. But winning an Eddie Award is still on my bucket list, and I'm going to savor every second here.

When we get to the spot where we pose for pictures, Roman gives my hand a squeeze and then lets go. He brings his lips close to my ear and breathes, "Knock 'em dead."

I walk to the mark and pose, cameras flashing all around. After adjusting my pose a few times, each time waiting for pictures to be taken, I wave Roman over to join me. I definitely want pictures of him beside me, looking so fine in his tux. He shakes his head, though, and calls out, "This is your moment to shine."

So I motion a bigger *get-over-here* arm gesture, and he heaves out a breath before straightening and walking to me. When he gets to me, I ask in a quiet voice, "Do you not want to be in pictures?"

Roman shakes his head. "No, it's fine."

We smile and pose, and then I thank the photographers and head toward the door leading into the hotel.

Once inside, we make our way into the Oregon Ballroom, and I immediately gasp, a tingling sensation spreading through my whole body. "My goodness, it's gorgeous."

Round tables fill the room, with floor-length silver tablecloths and blue napkins. The centerpieces are beautiful white and silver flowers with a miniature Eddie Award trophy rising from the center. The back of the stage is an impressive structure with tall, textured plexiglass windows with blue and purple lights behind. An attendant leads us to our seats, which are perfect. Close to the stage and facing it so we won't have to turn our chairs around when the ceremony starts.

Once I set my handbag at my seat, Roman and I go around the room, chatting with all the other attendees—many of whom are YouTubers I know who create many different genres of video content—until everyone arrives and it's time for the meal to be served.

I lean in close to Roman as we sit at our table. "Is everything okay? You've been seeming really distant and hesitant all evening."

"Everything is fine." He gives me a full, beautiful smile. "Enjoy your evening! You've worked hard for this."

By the time our waiter clears away our salads, it becomes even more clear that something is up with Roman. He still isn't being himself, and I can't seem to think of anything else. Did he get bad news? Did something go wrong with the investors? Is this the shield he had up when we first met about the interviews, or is this something else?

"For the lady," the waiter says as he places the entrée I chose in front of me, "wild-caught northwest salmon with roasted yellow beets, foraged mushrooms, and fried Brussel sprouts. And for the gentleman," he places a plate in front of Roman, "Painted Hills Ranch grass-fed grilled ribeye steak with potato puree, winter squash, and a demi-glace."

I look up at the waiter. "Thank you. This looks delicious."

During the meal, Roman and I chat with our table mates, one of whom is also up for an award but in a different category than I am. We mostly talk about the awards, our shows, and the roles the others at the table play.

Roman takes a sip of his drink. "So, what kinds of perks come from winning an Eddie?"

His question is aimed at Tatum, the woman at our table who also has a YouTube channel, so she answers. "I've seen Eddie winners get more than a million new subscribers. These awards can give you so much exposure that it leads to interviews, guest spots on other big channels, and sometimes even book deals."

I glance at Roman. Why does it seem like he isn't okay with that?

When all of the entrées have been cleared from the tables and all of the desserts—cheesecake with a blackberry sauce drizzled over it—are served, the ceremony starts with the organizers giving a few speeches. Then it's time for the awards themselves.

I've been thrilled to be a finalist. It has already given me a significant boost in subscribers and views of all of my videos. That, in itself, has been amazing. I haven't even let myself dream that I might win because I don't want my hopes dashed. This is my first year as a finalist, and creators are rarely bestowed with the award their first year.

I totally and completely think I'll be cool as a tall glass of milk when they start announcing the finalists in my category. With zero expectation of winning, that's how it's supposed to be, right? I know and admire all four of the other finalists, so my plan is just to cheer on whichever of my peers is announced as the winner.

Yet my heart is pounding and my breathing is shallow, making me feel lightheaded. Roman gives my hand a squeeze, so I look over at him. His confident smile is just what I need to convince my body to take a few normal breaths.

"And the winner is…" One of the two presenters behind the podium opens an envelope and pulls out the card inside. She leans in close to the microphone. "Bex Sterling with *Bexlandia*!"

Did I really just hear my name? Is it a fluke? Did they say the wrong name? Everyone at my table is motioning for me to stand up or go to the front, so I stand in a daze. Roman gives my hand one last squeeze, and I make my way to the stage to give an acceptance speech I didn't even begin to plan.

CHAPTER 18
Roman

FOR AS SURPRISED as Bex was when they called out her name as the winner, she sure seems prepared when she walks to the podium to give her acceptance speech. Maybe she's just that good at public speaking without preparing.

As I watch her on the stage, talking about why she started *Bexlandia* and about all the people who support her in her dream, I start to grasp what a monumental feat she has accomplished. My heart swells with pride. What she has achieved is rather incredible, and I am so impressed with everything that she is and everything she's done. I'm glad I've gotten this glimpse into a business I hadn't known much about at all until I met Bex.

She thanks the people who were instrumental in her getting the award—like her sisters and her roommates, who are regularly a part of her show, and especially Nikki, who makes magic out of what Bex hands her. And, of course, her nephew videographer, Enoch.

"And I need to thank Roman Powell, who is with me here tonight. Against his better judgment, he said yes to a series of four interviews and a whole lot of things neither of us expected. Like being chased down by a murderous deer who felt the need to protect his territory, being attacked by a blanket-shrouded mannequin, and being here together tonight."

The audience all chuckles before she goes on to finish her speech.

How am I simultaneously feeling win-the-Powerball lucky to be Bex's plus one for such an important award and so uneasy that she is making our relationship public? With how far the memes of people "shipping" us have spread, I can't imagine how much the news of us actually dating will spread.

———

I walk arm-in-arm with Bex into the Columbia Room, where the after-party is being held. The room is smaller but still grand, less elegant but more festive, and the lights are lower but flashing more. Like a nightclub, but although I can feel the bass in my chest, it isn't so loud that conversation is obliterated. A bar and refreshments table sits at the back of the room, with small standing-height tables dotting the outer edge of the room.

I enjoy going around with Bex to talk to creators she has met at conferences or conventions, ones she has chatted with online but not in person, as well as those she has just admired from afar. This is so different from the business receptions and parties I go to. The mood here is more light and fun. I'm guessing that the people here are more in direct competition with each other than I am with the business friends I get together with, yet there doesn't seem to be an air of competition here. It's filled with people who are all trying to build one another up. I've never seen anything like it.

"Jules!" Bex says as she moves around a crowd to hug someone she is obviously friends with. I feel like I should know her, too, and not knowing her exposes a huge hole in my pop culture knowledge.

Bex introduces me to her.

"So good to meet you," Jules says as she shakes my hand. "I have a racquetball background, too, and I've also been accused of hitting a pickleball a little too hard."

"You watched my show?" Bex asks.

"Of course I did! I love your show. And I've been a fan of Roman's ever since his *Business Success* interview, so I doubly couldn't miss it."

The three of us chat for a few minutes. I'm really starting to enjoy myself and forget about all the worries that have been creeping in.

Until I see the two photographers taking pictures. I turn my back toward them, hoping I can just use that tactic all night.

"Anyway, I am thrilled you won," Jules says. "You are going to be amazed at how much more visible you'll be. I nearly doubled my subscriber count the year I won."

"Doubled!"

"Yeah. It was insane."

One of the cameramen has made it to our section of the room, so I move around to Bex's other side to still have my back to the man. Bex shoots me a confused look but keeps the conversation going.

Then, she looks out to the people dancing in the middle of the room and turns to me. "Come dance with me."

I join her, but I definitely don't feel at home on the dance floor, dancing to the fast music. Sure, I was great at the choreographed dance routines of my youth, but it doesn't really translate into real-world fast dancing. The business get-togethers I go to never involve dancing to fast music, and it always makes me feel like a remote control toy robot whose controller is in the hands of a toddler.

The thought of the people I normally hang out with being someplace like this is laughable. They're all a bunch of hard-working CEOs and business consultants and strategists. They all seem to think that the only way to be successful is to work all the time. If they see pictures of me here, dancing like I've lost the ability to control my own arms and legs in a place that looks more like a club than a respectable business gathering, half of them are never going to let me live it down. The other half are going to quietly lose all respect for me and make underhanded comments about it.

It's not that my friends never have fun—they do. When they schedule it, and always in more respectable ways. Like playing golf. Or going yachting. Or having donuts brought into the office on National Donut Day.

Having pictures of me, trying to dance, out there for

everyone to see is not an option. So I try to subtly move us toward the end of the room away from the photographer.

Is this going to be my life if I keep dating Bex, especially now that she's won? Am I going to have to constantly try to keep our relationship and everything we do together from being a big thing online?

Guiding Bex toward the other end of the room, though, is a bad idea, because it leads us right down to the area where the second photographer is. And now that I'm closer, I see that this one is the photographer who took my pictures that they placed alongside my interview and on the cover of *Business Success* magazine. And not too far away is Tarak, the man who interviewed me, talking with one of the winners in a different category. I quickly move to where a crowd of about five people blocks us from the interviewer's line of sight.

Of course, Tarak and his cameraman are here for this—all of the finalists are business owners, after all. Even though I hadn't expected them to be here, even a little bit, it makes sense.

I definitely need to stay away from them. From the email I got from Tarak a month after that issue came out, I know that the issue with me on the cover had their second biggest circulation numbers. If they see me, they will want to talk to me, and they might want to mention something about me being here with Bex. Even if they only mention it on their social media and not in their magazine, it will get back to my dad. Anything related to *Business Success* will get back to him.

The words my dad said to me two nights ago are so fresh

they're still running in a constant loop in my head. How I made a fool of myself in Bex's interviews, and how he has never been more disappointed in me. How I'm not living up to the professionalism required of someone with the last name of Powell, and how any serious relationship needs to be with someone who has a respectable career, someone who will not bring down the Powell name.

Yet, here I am, two days later, at a ceremony where they give out awards for placing "simpleton content on a simpleton site." And the channel that won in her category is the channel where I "made a fool of myself" for all the world to see.

Tarak spots us and heads in our direction. So I do a spin move that takes us out of his line of sight.

Bex sees the interviewer, though, and apparently isn't fooled at all by what I've done. She stops right where she is, a hand on her hip. "What is up with you tonight?"

I try to act like my mind isn't full of everything I heard from my peers and my dad on Thursday night, but she isn't buying it. Instead, she grabs hold of my hand and leads me to the doors, out of the party, and into the triangular space just beyond.

"Why have you been such a jerk tonight? I wouldn't have pegged you as someone who would get jealous of another person's success, but maybe I was wrong."

"What? No. It's not that at all. I am so proud of you, and I'm so thrilled you won." I do not want to have this conversation with her tonight. Or ever. This is her night, and all of my frustrations about what everyone I know thinks about me dating Bex are irrelevant. So instead of bringing up any of that, I say, "I just don't want to be in a bunch of pictures that people are going to be posting online."

"You're embarrassed to be seen with me?"

"No." I say the word emphatically, and I think I mean it without any hesitation, but even I can hear the lie in that one single word. If I'm worried about what my business friends, my brothers, and my dad think about the two of us together, and what they will think of me because I'm here and dating her, then embarrassed to be seen with her is exactly what I am. "Let's just go back inside."

"No," she drags the word out, irritation clouding her features, "there's something you want to say but aren't saying. Spill it."

Why is she pushing a conversation that shouldn't be happening tonight?

"Now."

Frustration that has been building all night bursts free. "I am so happy and excited that you won the Eddie! I am. But, come on, Bex. Your job is about creating content that helps people procrastinate doing the more important things they should be doing."

I know it's a mistake the moment I say it and instantly regret it. "I'm sorry, Bex. That's not what I meant to say."

She is quiet for a long moment. Then, in an eerily calm voice, she says, "Maybe not, but I think it's the first honest thing you've said all night."

"No, I—" I reach a hand out to her, but she steps back.

"I know you don't want to be here, so you should just leave. I'll find my own ride home."

"No, Bex. This is your night. I'll stay."

She shakes her head. "I don't want you to."

Then she turns and walks away from me and back into the party. I stand in the hallway for several long moments, running my hand through my hair and trying to calm my breathing, cursing my own stupidity, and wishing I could redo this entire night.

CHAPTER 19

Bex

I HAVE both of my video cameras set up in the kitchen on tripods at different angles, both running. I'll use my cell phone video camera here and there, and then Nikki will piece everything together later. Standing in front of one of the cameras, I introduce the video.

"Hello, Bexlandians! Today on our *Hidden Inn Roomies* segment, we are going to tackle something that everyone with roommates has to tackle—cleaning! What's that? Boring, you say? Mundane? A game where you're on one team, your roommates are on the other, and penalties are getting called on everyone?

"Then you're not doing it right." I hold up my phone. "Step one to getting it right: set up a Spotify music list that you all agree on. Step two: gather everyone together for a cleaning party." I motion for my roommates to come into the video frame, and they all squeeze in, waving with elbow-length pink dish-scrubbing gloved hands and cleaning bottles. "Step three: blast music and clean!"

I start the music, and we all scatter to mostly different parts of the kitchen, dancing as we do. We haven't decided ahead of time who is going to clean what, so my audience gets to see all the negotiations on that, too. Addison and Ian pair up to clean out the fridge, and I'm glad that I have one of the cameras aimed at them. The looks on their faces are priceless as they open containers of food and smell them to see if they're still good.

I use my cell phone camera to catch the disagreement between Peyton and Timini on who should work on the counters, the big dining table, and the myriad smaller tables in the inn's big dining room, and who should tackle the big job of sweeping and mopping the expansive floors. Once they agree to split both, I turn off the camera on my phone and start on the dishes.

The music is energetic, everyone is dancing and singing along and having a great time as they work, and I really try to do the same. I dance a bit as I rinse off dishes and load the dishwasher, knowing I'm in the frame, but my mind wanders to Roman, and my having-a-blast expression slips.

Then, as I'm scrubbing the sink and the handle breaks right off the scrubber, I decide maybe I'm pouring a bit too much emotion into the job. I have to get my head back into the game. Addison and Ian have already grabbed both mops and have started mopping the big floor, even though Timini hasn't finished sweeping, so things are moving fast.

Within moments, Peyton finishes the last of the counter-tops, and Addison and Ian race into the space, seeing who can finish mopping first. It ends with all of us in the space between the back counter and the island, panting and grinning at the clean kitchen.

"And that's how it's done, folks," I say, and then turn off the camera. Then I chuck both pieces of the broken scrubber into the garbage can.

Addison's gaze goes from the garbage can to me. "Are you sure you should be filming segments right now?"

"Yes."

"I don't know, Bex," Peyton says. "It's only been three days, and you can't get over a relationship like yours and Roman's in three days."

I shake my head. "There's only so much administrative work I can do before my head explodes. And I need to keep busy to keep my mind off him."

Because if I don't, all I can do is think of him. About how much I enjoy being with him. How much I love brainstorming with him about our businesses. How much I enjoy laughing and doing fun things with him. The sweet look on his face right before he kisses me. The way he challenges and pushes me and is never, ever boring.

But being in the spotlight as much as I am isn't for everyone. Especially now that I've won the Eddie. I know that. I don't know why I haven't been cutting Roman more slack about it all along. Sure, he was super resistant to the interviews at the beginning, but he was so good at it and he seemed to deal with all the attention they brought just fine. So I assumed he was okay with it and never really talked with him about it.

Maybe I handled things wrong at the awards party and

overreacted. And maybe I under-reacted. I'm still so mad at him for the words he said. And not just for saying it, but for *thinking* it! For *believing* it. I need someone who will support me in my career, and not think it's trivial.

Maybe ending things with Roman is for the best. I remember very clearly all that Nikki went through after marrying a guy who was driven, opinionated, and stubborn, and I don't want to have to go through any of that. Maybe it's good we stopped dating before I got any more of my heart invested.

I *should* be relieved.

So why do I feel so awful?

"Whatever," I say as I remove one of the cameras from the tripod. "It's not like he's called, anyway."

When I turn back to my roommates/friends and see the looks of sorrow on their faces, I feel the tears welling up inside. I haven't cried in front of them at all. But as they surround me in a hug, the tears start falling freely, and I let myself cry.

CHAPTER 20

Roman

I COLLAPSE into the chair at the desk in my office at the end of a really long day. The end of a really long week, actually. I run my hands through my hair and then just sit, elbows on the table, hands holding my head.

I just *cannot* stop thinking about Bex. How have I managed to mess up the best thing I've ever had in my life?

I pull my laptop toward me, open a browser, and find her on YouTube. I got a notification earlier today that a new video was posted, so I push play on it. She has posted three new ones this week, along with two Facebook Live videos. I've watched them all. Each one is torture, but I can't seem to stay away. I miss her smile. Her personality. Her voice. Her determination, spunk, and drive. I miss *all* of it.

I startle when Everly pokes her head in. "Whatcha doing here still, Boss?"

I lift a shoulder in a shrug. "You?"

"I forgot my lunch bag and didn't want to leave it here

getting gross all weekend." She sits down in the chair across from me and sighs. "Are you watching one of her videos again?"

I turn the laptop toward Everly. "Look how happy she is."

She looks at the screen for a moment, which is paused on Bex's face, then looks back at me. "And you're wondering why she's so happy when you aren't? You want to know why it isn't wrecking her the way it's wrecking you?"

I am. I'm too ashamed to admit it out loud, though. I *should* be happy that she's happy. I don't want her to be as miserable as I am.

"I don't know, Roman. Maybe she isn't. I mean, I've seen you fake it pretty well this week, too. And she probably filmed this before the awards ceremony." We both stay silent for a few moments and then she says, "Have you called her yet?"

I shake my head. "Those words I said to her—I would've only expected them to have come out of my dad's mouth. But they didn't—*I* said them, and it was bad. Some things just aren't forgivable."

"I don't believe that."

"Bex doesn't have any reason to forgive me for it. Or to believe that I didn't actually mean them."

"Well, then it sounds like you need to first make sure you don't actually believe the words you said, and second, find a way to convince Bex that she should forgive you." Everly stands up. "And when you get to the part of convincing Bex, if you need any help, I will gladly do whatever you need. Anything to get my old boss back."

I chuckle. "Thanks, Everly. Have a good weekend."

She nods, then turns and leaves. I pull the laptop to me again and start scrolling through the comments section, like I've been doing ever since I was such a jerk last Saturday. And like with every video, I quickly find comments from people who've been helped by Bex. *Many, many* comments. Like the one that's just five comments down on this video.

Thank you so much for your videos, Bex! Not long ago, I was stuck in an awful job with an awful boss, working for an awful company. Your videos taught me how to be brave and convinced me that I could be. I took some huge steps that I would've never dared to take if it weren't for your channel, and my life is so much better now than I ever thought possible. You changed my life, and I will be forever grateful.

And plenty of ones like the comment just after it.

I have a very high-stress job, and if I want to stay healthy, when I come home, I need something to help me unwind. Your videos always do that for me, so thank you! I'm pretty sure my doctor would thank you for saving a life, haha. I know I do.

I don't know if I ever would've thought that Bex's career choice was frivolous or unimportant or nothing more than a way to make people procrastinate important things on my own. I like to think that I wouldn't have.

But between having my business peers razz me about the wisdom in doing the interviews and my dad's lecture about what's expected of a Powell and how thoroughly Bex doesn't fit that requirement, I definitely thought it. And I feel like a jerk for having done so.

But now, on my sixth night of watching her videos and reading the comments from the people whose lives she has changed, I realize how very, *very* wrong I was that night almost a week ago. The night when she was being professionally celebrated for the contributions she had made, no less.

I want to be with Bex. More than anything. But I don't deserve her. Before last Saturday, I saw myself as my own man. It isn't until I look back on everything now that I realize how much I've been letting other people in my life drive how I react to things, and even how I think about things.

And as long as I'm doing that, I am never going to deserve her.

CHAPTER 21

Bex

I DON'T HAVE any grandparents, and that's what I really need right now. A grandma who will feed me something sugary and fattening, rub my back in a circle, and spout wisdom. So I'm going to have to borrow Ian's grandma. I text Shirley, and she responds with a quick *Yes! Come ear. We want to see you!*

I open the kitchen door to Ian's house—the one his grandma and her friend, Carol, now live in—to the smell of brownies and the hellos of five women. All of whom get out of their seats and come to give me a hug.

"Wow!" I say, hugging each of them back. "I didn't know I'd be getting the entire origami club. Or this many hugs."

"Well, dear," Shirley says, offering me a seat and a bowl with a brownie and a scoop of vanilla ice cream, "a breakup on the level of yours and Roman's requires lots of hugs. Every single one of us has been there."

Meera nods. "Frances has been there three times."

"That's why I gave you the extra-long hug, honey," Frances says.

"I set her up with two of those," Brenda says. "Want me to set you up with someone? I have a grandson—"

Ian's grandma, Shirley, starts rubbing circles on my back. "She doesn't want to be set up on a date. She's still working on this one. How's the recovery coming, sweetheart?"

I sigh and take a bite of the brownie. The heat of the brownie next to the cold of the ice cream, all of it so sweet and so delicious, is just what I need. Then I look up at the women seated around the table, each of them showing enough wrinkles to prove how experienced in life they are, each with a pile of colored papers and half-folded creations in front of them.

"It's been a week, and it's just not getting any better. He was the only guy I never got bored of. I think I could be with him my entire life and not ever get bored of him. And now he's gone. And I just feel like…" I swirl my spoon in the part of the ice cream that's melting. "I feel like I lost something truly great, you know? How do I get over someone like that?"

"How long have you known him?" Carol asks.

"If you count since Ian's and Addison's wedding, then about three months. But we did our first interview two-and-a-half months ago. We've dated for about two." Which is about a month and a week longer than any other relation-ship I've ever had. Two months might not feel like a long relationship to some people, but it's an eternity for me.

"Well," Carol says, "I've seen you both enough that I'm going to tell you right now you're asking the wrong question. You shouldn't be asking how to get over him—you should be asking how you can get him back."

I give a humorless breath of a laugh. "No—that train has left the station." Then I take another bite of the brownie because it's really good and it feels like a warm hug in itself.

"Why has the train left?" Brenda asks.

"Because I already made the decision. And if you heard what he said that night, you would've made the same decision, too. Just like with every decision I make, I go with my gut and stick with it. It has served me well so far."

Carol snorts. "Just because you're decisive doesn't mean you're always right."

"True," Shirley says. "Remember how we planned that backyard barbecue with all of us and we were trying to decide if we should cancel because it looked like rain? You decided we should keep it and wouldn't turn back, even when it was obvious that you should. Remember where that got you? In a soaking wet outfit with soaking wet hamburger buns. Sticking to that decision didn't help you then, and it isn't going to help you now."

My cell phone buzzes, so I take it out of my pocket. It's a text from my sister.

Nikki: Where are you?

I send a quick response back.

Bex: At Ian's grandma's, having brownies and ice cream.

The moment I tap send, I remember we were supposed to meet to go over some business items. So I send a second text.

Bex: So sorry! Are you at the inn looking for me? I'll be right over.

Nikki's response comes just as quickly.

Nikki: NO. STAY THERE. I'm coming where the brownies are.

"Shirley filled us in on what happened between you two," Meera says as soon as I slip the phone back into my pocket. "Men do stupid things sometimes. It's a fact of life. So does everyone. The point is that people do stupid things and you forgive them. You let them learn and grow and become better. If you didn't, no relationship would ever survive."

I could forgive Roman. In fact, I'm pretty sure that I already have. It doesn't mean I'm not still hurt, but I sometimes say rude things without really meaning to, too. I can let him learn and grow and become better, no problem. But does that mean I should continue to date him? I'm not sure.

Nikki knocks twice on the kitchen door before coming inside and moaning as she accepts the bowl with a brownie and ice cream from Shirley. She immediately sits down and eats a big spoonful of the dessert, mumbling "Thanks" and "*Mmm*, so good" around her mouthful.

And, even if she doesn't realize it, her presence reminds me *exactly* why I can't continue to date Roman.

"What was that expression?" Frances asks.

I look at her in confusion.

"You looked at Nikki like she has something to do with this."

"What?" Nikki says with a mouthful of ice cream. "I didn't have anything to do with it."

"No, I saw it, too," Meera says.

Nikki swallows. "Tell them I didn't."

I let out a huge breath of air. "All my sisters are driven and have strong opinions and even stronger wills."

"That's so true," Nikki says. "You should see what it's like just trying to decide where to go to lunch. And by the way, Bex is the most driven of us all. Oh, but did you notice? She said *all* our sisters. See? So whatever she's talking about, it isn't my fault."

I laugh. "It isn't her fault. It's just that all my sisters figured out that they couldn't marry a guy who was also driven with strong opinions and a strong will, except for Nikki. The guy she married was as strong-willed and driven as they come, and it was awful."

"Okay, that part's true. Between dating, engagement, marriage, and divorce, four years of my life: down the crapper. Wait. What does this have to do with you?"

"Well, obviously," I say, "it doesn't work for people like us to be with a guy like that. You married someone kind and sweet and easygoing and everything is rainbows and lollipops for you. Roman is totally driven and strong-willed and has strong opinions. So we would never work out. We'd just end up like you and Brant and waste years of our lives."

"*That's* what you think?" Nikki asks. "Wow, so it really *is* my fault. I would've never guessed."

"No, it's the opposite of your fault. I'm learning from your mistakes so I don't have to make the same ones."

Nikki turns in her seat to face me. "Bex. Brant and I didn't work out because he is a Class A—" she glances at the women in the room and amends whatever she was going to say "—Jerk. *Not* because he's driven and opinionated. Sure, Dylan and I are pretty much the best couple on the planet, but that's got nothing to do with how accommodating and flexible he is and everything to do with him *not* being a jerk. Do you know who else is *not* a jerk? Roman. Well, except at that party where he definitely was a jerk. But the rest of the time? Not so much."

Could it be possible that Roman *isn't* the wrong kind of guy for me? I feel a strange flutter of hope that I haven't felt in the week since the Eddie Awards.

But that doesn't change the fact that he showed that he didn't respect my job, and therefore didn't respect me.

Nikki takes another bite of brownie and ice cream, and then mumbles. "Sorry—I'm really pregnant and this is really good." She swallows her bite before pointing her spoon at me. "Maybe the reason you never stay interested in a guy longer than two or three dates is because the kind of guy that we all married isn't the kind of guy you need. You've stayed interested—*extremely* interested—in Roman for longer than I thought you'd ever stay interested in a guy, and based on the way you're dealing"—she clears her throat—"or *not* dealing with the breakup tells me that you'll likely be interested for the long haul."

"Besides, sweetie," Shirley says, placing a hand on my arm, "you've always struck me as someone who's going to be a formidable half of a power couple. You don't become a power couple with someone who bends like a willow tree. You do it with someone who's an oak."

I really have never thought about it like that before. But looking back, I realize how much Roman has pushed and challenged me over the past couple of months. We have pushed and challenged each other, actually. So many times over the past several weeks, we've brainstormed about each of our businesses, coming up with new ideas. Some, I've been nervous about trying, but he encouraged me, and I've accomplished things I didn't think I could. It has exhilarated me.

I've been more productive and have been willing to take bigger risks than ever before. I've dreamed bigger dreams and I'm going for them. I won an Eddie, and I know with all my heart that I couldn't have done it without him.

Maybe I need to dial back my commitment to sticking with a decision once I've made it. At least when it comes to Roman. But only if I feel like he truly does respect my job and isn't embarrassed to be with me.

And I'm not sure those things are true. If he does respect my job and isn't embarrassed to be with me, will I ever even know? And is he interested in a relationship with me? Because he hasn't called in a week, and that's not really what a guy who's interested does.

CHAPTER 22

Roman

I'M on my way to my dad's office when my phone rings. I was hoping to catch him at home, even though it's a longer drive than his office is, but of course, he has to go in to work on a Saturday. He's probably even wearing a suit.

I glance at my phone—it's my friend, Ian. If it was anyone else, I might ignore the call. I press to answer through my car's Bluetooth. "Hello?"

"Hey, buddy. How are you?"

"Feeling good for the first time in a week, actually."

"That's... not what I was expecting."

"Me neither. Especially because I'm on my way to talk to my dad."

"When is that *ever* a good thing?"

"When I've decided that I'm going to go tell him off. I am a twenty-nine-year-old man. Not only have I lived with zero support from him since college, but I am the CEO of a company I built from the ground up. He doesn't get a say in what I do or who I date."

"I so wish I could be there when you tell him that."

I chuckle. "I wish you could, too." I pause a moment, wondering if I should ask, then decide I want to know too badly to care if I should ask or not. "How's Bex?"

"Miserable. She's a million times better with you, and you're a million times better with her. Addi and I both hate seeing her so miserable. Please tell me you're going to do something about it."

"I am," I say as I pull into the parking lot of my dad's office building. "I'm going to do absolutely everything within my power. I have to convince her to give me another chance."

"Oh, good. Because I care about you both way too much for you to not work this out."

I take a deep breath. "Well, when you mess up as badly as I did, I think it's going to take a *lot* to work this out. And I may need your help."

"You've got it. Anything."

I look up at the building in front of me. "I need to go talk to my dad first, and then I'll call you back."

Normally, I would spend the entire walk into the building, the ride on the elevator, the walk down the hallway of the executive suite, and waiting outside his office dreading whatever talk we were about to have. Even if I have good news, talks with my dad are rarely all good.

But this time, I walk with confidence. Sure, I'm uncertain how my dad will react, and I know it won't be well, but I also feel the power that comes from making a decision so fully and gaining the knowledge that nothing can sway me from that decision. And that power fuels me.

Because over the past week, I've realized that I'm the most myself when I'm around Bex. I've been showing a modified, filtered and concealed, scrubbed and polished, masked version of myself that I've hidden behind for so long that I had forgotten what it's like to truly be me. The time we spent filming the videos and dating afterward has been the most *me* I've felt in a long time. And as it turns out, I like who I am.

And Bex is the one who has managed to pull me out from behind that front and make me feel like I don't have to pretend. I don't know how she managed to do it while filming for an audience of two million, but she did.

As grateful as I am for that, it's only a small fraction of why I love her. I want to be able to tell her all the reasons and keep telling her throughout our lives. Before I do, though, I need to set some clear, strong boundaries with my father.

It's been a while since I've been in my father's office on a Saturday, and everything feels so empty. His assistant, Susan, isn't here, of course, so my dad answers the knock on his door himself.

"Roman. This is a surprise."

"Do you have a minute? I want to talk."

He glances at the laptop on his desk, then must decide whatever he's working on can wait. "Sure. Come on in. But if this is about the trip, don't bother."

I close the door and stand in front of my dad. "It's not about the trip, Dad."

"Oh?"

"It's about me. And Bex Sterling. And about LivenUP."

Instead of sitting down behind his desk, my dad just leans against the front of it, crossing his arms.

"You and Mom raised me to be a good person"—okay, that part was mostly my mom, but I'm trying to start the conversation in a way that won't make my dad defensive—"and to be respectable. I am grateful for that. And I'm grateful that you've built the Powell name to be what it is.

"But through it all, I need to be who I am. And it will not always be in a way that you approve."

My dad just stands there, arms crossed, not interrupting. So I continue.

"I am going to run my business my way. I am going to make the decisions I feel are right for it and the ones I feel good about making. I am not going to let your approval in the form of words or a trip you've been hanging over my head influence my decisions. I am the CEO, and that means I make the calls."

His face is stoic, giving nothing away. I can't tell if he's agreeing with anything or getting more furious as I go on. But it doesn't matter, because I'm not going to stop until I'm finished.

"Next, you are wrong about Bex. *So very wrong.* She does not post 'simpleton content on a simpleton site.' And even if she did, there's a need for that, too. What she does is produce well-thought-out and well-planned segments that draw in millions. I have run into countless people who she has helped in one way or another through her channel. But even if you don't respect what she creates, you would respect the grace, skill, prowess, and professionalism with which she runs her business.

"But Bex as a businessperson is only a small part of who she is, and who she is as a person blows all that out of the water. She is generous in sharing her time, talents, knowledge, and money. She cares about people and will do anything needed to help. She can organize anything from big crowds to a rowdy bunch of kids to a successful business built on her image alone. She is kind and fun and thoughtful and strong, and she is deserving of your awe and respect in all facets of her life. If the Powell family is lucky enough to have her join our ranks, *she would bring us up.* Not the other way around.

"Now, I don't know if I can win her back, but I definitely know I can't if I only put forth the face I feel like I'm supposed to show. I can only do it if my true self is unapologetically coming through. So that's what I'm going to do.

"Now you can disagree with all of that, but it doesn't matter, because it's not going to influence me anymore. I am still going to go forward living my life the way I think I should, and I am still going to move heaven and earth to get Bex back in my life. And I'm going to spend my life being the kind of man who is worthy of her. The kind she'll want to have in her life always."

A smile plays at the corner of my dad's mouth, and I wonder if it's because he's thought of a retort that he's about to blast me with. But then he gives a single nod. "I won't stand in your way."

Is that genuine or passive-aggressive? It seems genuine, which makes no sense.

He stands up straight and walks around to the back of his desk, then meets my eyes. "If you were willing to walk away from someone you were interested in because I—or anyone else—said you should, or because someone cast doubts on your relationship, then either she wasn't the right one or you weren't ready for her. If you're willing to storm in here and stand up to me to fight for her, then I think you probably both have what it takes to last."

I just stare at him, dumbfounded.

Richmond Powell IV, D.B.A., takes a seat and picks up the pen he was probably using before I came into his office. "But I'm still going to tell you every time I see you making a decision that I think is an idiot move."

Fair enough. I give him a nod. "And I will listen and follow your advice if it rings true and ignore it completely if it doesn't." I'm not about to let him bully me into a decision ever again. "Now, if you'll excuse me, I need to go set something into motion that you are definitely not going to approve of."

I don't wait for his response. I walk out of his office with my chin up and shoulders back, ready to thrust a fist into the air. This is the first time I've stood up to him and he's backed down. I hadn't even imagined that was possible.

It makes me feel freer to make my own decisions than I've ever been before.

That's one thing down, but I'm far from finished. I still have several people I need to meet with, including Tarak from *Business Success* magazine, to begin to undo the damage I've caused and make things right.

When I think back to the man I was a week ago when I

ruined everything, it amazes me how different I feel now. I sent a clear message to Bex a week ago that I didn't respect her job and that I didn't want to be seen with her. It's time to show her how I really feel, and that I want the world—but most importantly, her—to know it.

CHAPTER 23

Bex

"I CAN'T BELIEVE I let you all talk me into coming here," I say to my roommates as we put our lanyards on over our heads that hold our name badges and the *PNW Open for Business* convention logo. I look around at the massive lobby of the Oregon Convention Center. Normally, I like being around this many people. Right now, though, I don't want to socialize.

I don't even want to talk shop in all the lectures or with the business product owners, which has never happened before. But everyone said that coming would be good "roommate bonding" and would "get my mind off of things." I'm pretty sure they're wrong.

"Should we go check out the exhibit hall?" Timini asks, eyeing the big doors leading into the vendor area.

Addison glances at her watch. "As long as we don't stay too long. I want to catch some of the programming."

The five of us start going up and down the aisles in the

exhibit hall, checking out all the displays from companies selling products that help business owners. Everything I see reminds me of Roman. The business planning software reminds me of our brainstorming sessions. The breakroom furniture reminds me of sitting on the bench in Tsuru Island at the park together, eating dessert. The phone system reminds me of him being so sweet and helping me get past the panic of an imminent bird attack. It all makes my heart hurt.

"Anyone want to catch a panel or lecture? I need to…" I point toward the exit, but can't find a way to end the sentence. They all seem to get it, though.

"I want to!" Peyton says. "Ooh. There's one starting in ten minutes." She pulls out her convention schedule, and we all crowd in to look at it.

"That one," Ian says, pointing at the one on social media marketing. "I am terrible at that. Anyone else?"

Four minutes later, we're all filing into the big room numbered *A105-106* and finding seats. I sit down between Peyton and Timini and pull out my notebook. Instead of being a panel discussion, it's actually Tarak, the interviewer from *Business Success* who I spoke with at the awards ceremony, pulling in one panelist at a time and asking them questions.

Which hurts in its own way, since Tarak and *Business Success* played a big hand in Roman and me getting together in the first place. My viewers wouldn't have even known who Roman was if it weren't for that article.

It's probably a really interesting conversation. I just can't seem to focus. Instead, I start doodling. At first, it's just in the margins of the notebook. Before long, my doodles cover the entire page, and I have no idea what the speakers have been saying. I thought my mind was just blank—not thinking about Roman at all—but then I notice that most of my doodles resemble Roman's company logo, one of his app's logos, or something from one of our interviews together. Oh, look—that one is like the avocado-shaped cats we painted in our class.

I've been blindsided by how much I miss him. I have never in my life missed a guy before. There have always been plenty of interesting things to move on to. But I miss just being in the same room as Roman so much it physically hurts.

I hear the name "Roman Powell" over the microphone, and my head jerks up. Roman is walking right onto the stage and taking the seat next to Tarak.

I look at my friends surrounding me so we can all share in the shock at seeing him on stage, but none of them look nearly as surprised as I am. I lean over to Timini. "Did you know he was on this panel?"

"Shh," she says. "I'm listening."

So I listen, too.

"A lot of you might recognize our next panelist. Roman Powell became much more of a household name when he made the cover of our magazine and it became our second best-selling issue of all time."

"It's good to see you again, Tarak."

I cannot believe how much I miss hearing that voice. Seeing him and hearing him again grabs at my throat.

"You, too. I'm glad you finally responded to my email to join me on the stage here."

Roman chuckles and rubs the back of his neck. "Better late than never, right?"

I miss running my own fingers on the back of his neck. I miss touching that spot where his hair curls just slightly right in front of his ear. And seeing the way his mouth curls up on one side when he's amused, kind of like it is right now.

"Now, your company was rocking before the *Business Success* issue with you on it. Which is why, of course, you were on it in the first place. But your business has exploded since then. You've had a new product release, Nudge Out." Tarak turns to the audience. "Which you should all get right now. Roman told me about it in our interview, and the second it went live, I downloaded it. It got me to try synchronized swimming which, I've got to say, was much more difficult and more fun than I ever would have guessed. I'd like you to tell us, Roman, what you did to capitalize on the success of that issue."

"You know the old saying that the three most important things in a business are location, location, location? When you have a digital offering, I think it's more along the lines of excellent employees, luck, and finding your target audience. Thanks in part to a very persistent and very skilled social media and marketing manager at my company, and in large part to a lot of different pieces falling into place, I managed to get an interview with the amazing Bex Sterling of *Bexlandia*. A four-part interview, actually. She has a massive fan base that just happened to be my target audience, and those interviews helped so much to get the word out about our new product."

There's something about the way he says things. They're just more charming when they come out of Roman's mouth. He's so confident and relaxed up there, connecting with the audience so well. I never would have guessed that from our first couple of meetings before the interviews, but he has gotten more and more at home with it every time. It makes me long for the time when we were bantering together in front of the camera.

I can't leave. I want to see him again so badly that I can't pass up this chance to see him shine on stage. But I know that watching him and being reminded about all the things I love about him is going to wreck me later.

"Oh, that's a great show," Tarak says. "I was there nearly two weeks ago when she won an Eddie for it. Everyone, if you're not already watching *Bexlandia* on YouTube, you really should check it out because she is a savant at social media. I actually interviewed Bex that night. We're having a special issue with creators of digital content come out in about two months that she'll be in, and we're pretty excited about that."

He turns back to Roman. "But I saw you, too, that night, and it didn't look like things were going so well for you."

"No, Tarak, they were not."

Oh, how awkward. I can't believe Tarak is asking him about that. Especially since Roman didn't want anyone to know that we'd been dating. He probably wants to exit the stage pretty quickly right about now.

I want to exit the room, too, because I don't want to relive the moment when things went so downhill for us. I look to the left and the right. How did I manage to get stuck in the middle of the row? We're toward the back of the room, but there are several hundred people in it, so there's no way I can escape without making a scene.

Roman looks down for a few moments before he looks out at the audience. "You know how it is when you're running your business and things are going decently well but you still don't have everything figured out yet, and suddenly everyone is giving you advice?"

The audience is chuckling and nodding. They've probably all been exactly there. I know I have.

"And some of it is actually incredibly terrible advice, but you don't know that yet, so you follow it and everything goes wrong?"

More nodding from the audience, this time a little more emphatically.

"It was kind of like that, only so much worse. And instead of a business, it was a woman I'm in love with. And instead of just being clueless, I was also a jerk."

My eyes go wide, and I turn to Peyton and then to Timini, Addison, and Ian. Did Roman really just say he's in love with me?

"I assume this woman we are talking about is Bex Sterling?"

Roman nods. "It is."

"And did I hear you right? You love her."

Roman lets out a breath and shakes his head like he's still in disbelief over it all. "It's pretty impossible not to fall in love with someone like Bex."

I gasp, and my hand flies to my mouth. My eyes start to water, and I blink fast, trying to clear my vision so I don't miss one second of seeing Roman.

"I'm impressed—it takes a lot of bravery to get up here and announce something like that to everyone."

"Actually, it doesn't. I want the whole world to know. I want my peers to know. I want my family, my employees, my friends, and all the Bexlandians to know that I am in love with Bex Sterling. It isn't brave of me to say it now; it was cowardly of me to not say it before."

Tears spill onto my face. He loves me. And not only that, he wants everyone to know.

"When you say 'before,' were you talking about that night at the awards?" When Roman nods, Tarak asks, "So what changed?"

"Me. Like I said, I was a jerk, and I was rude, and most importantly, I was wrong. It took a lot of intense soul-searching, setting boundaries with certain people, choosing which voices I'm going to listen to, coming to some realizations, and making a plan going forward."

Tarak nods. "Sometimes when we mess up badly, that's what it takes. Tell me: if Bex were here now, what would you say to her?"

Roman looks right out into the audience. "I would tell her that she's the most amazing woman I've ever known and that I admire everything about her. She's organized, patient, dreams big, sets goals, works hard, and does everything she can to reach those goals. I have now watched nearly every video she has ever posted, and I can say without a doubt that she has created an amazing channel with incredible content, and I have so much respect for what she does.

"No matter how busy she is, she'll drop everything to help out someone in need. Whether it's someone wanting advice while she's waiting in line, someone needing a shoulder to cry on, an email asking for help, or her nephew, who needed an adult to attend a sleepover at the aviary with him when his mom was out of town. Bex stepped in even though she's terrified of birds. She's willing to help out regardless.

"She's got strong opinions and she isn't afraid to share them. Even when her opinion is the unpopular one. She fights for what she thinks is right. She stands up for the little guy. She pushes people to be better and brings out the best in them. She has definitely brought out the best in me." He chuckles, shaking his head. "I mean, before her, my personality only came out in my choice of socks."

Tarak and the rest of the audience laugh, and so do I as I wipe away the tears spilling onto my cheeks.

"I love her completely. I want the whole world to know it. And I am hoping that it's not too late to fully apologize and make up for the mistakes I've made."

The audience lets out a collective "Awww!"

I can't stay seated any longer. There's too much space separating me and Roman, and I need there to not be space. Tarak looks out into the audience and makes eye contact with me. He doesn't look at all surprised that I'm here—almost like he'd known I was here and where I was sitting all along. He gives me a single nod, like he agrees that it's time for me to come up.

I start trying to get to the center aisle as Tarak says to Roman, "Do you wonder what she would say if she were here?" Then he turns to the crowd. "Audience, what do you think?"

They all cheer and clap as each person between me and the aisle moves bags, shifts their knees to the side, or stands up to let me pass. I'm pretty sure I step on a toe or two, and even hit my arm against the back of a guy's head at some point, but I finally make it to the center aisle.

I rush toward the stage, wondering how I'm going to get up on it when one of the event center ushers holds both arms out in the direction of the stairs. I don't even have time to step into the front aisle, let alone head for the stairs, before Roman jumps off the stage and meets me, front and center.

His face is so full of love and apology and hope that I reach for it, putting a hand on each side of his face, and then crushing my lips against his. I'm vaguely aware of a roar of approval coming from the crowd, but it falls away. Off in the distance. All I can focus on is Roman's arms around me, his lips against mine, a confirmation that everything he said is true, along with a promise of the future.

When we finally break for air, we keep our foreheads together, breathing hard. A smile spreads across Roman's face, and I can't help the one that spreads across mine. Besides the cameras that are filming all sessions of the conference, I'm sure that there are more than a few cell phones out, recording our reunion.

"You just kissed me in front of a very large crowd."

"I hope it goes even more viral than the memes. I want everyone to know I love you."

"And I want them all to know that I love you just as much."

The smile on his face is so beautiful. I want to stare at it for hours.

Roman glances at the doors at the other end of the center aisle. "What do you say we go find someplace else to be?"

I nod and we both turn to give Tarak a thank you. Then I put my hand in Roman's, threading my fingers through his, and we walk to the doors together.

CHAPTER 24

Roman

I STEP out into the lobby with Bex before the current sessions end, so the area has a lot fewer people in it now than it will in just a few minutes. I lead her down the wide halls to an ice cream kiosk I found earlier. In hopes that everything would work out in my interview, I'd stopped by before and already ordered and paid, asking the two people working the kiosk to have them ready at about this time.

When Bex and I step up to the kiosk, the young man working grins as he hands the ice creams to us. They didn't have Ben & Jerry's flavors, but they do have blueberry, raspberry, and vanilla, so I'd asked them to put the three flavors together in a bowl for Bex and to make a chocolate chip cookie dough bowl for me. I slip the guy an extra $10 tip to say thanks.

A few minutes later, we're sitting on a bench in a secluded little spot I'd found earlier where we can talk. It overlooks a patch of grass, a few shrubs, and is shaded by a giant tree. We're both quiet for a moment as we take our first bites of ice cream, and then I turn to her.

"What I said in there was just a start in my plan to make things up to you. I really am sorry for the way I behaved and the things I said. I would also like to apologize for taking nearly two weeks to say that. There were so many things I was wrong about, and I wanted to make sure I got them right first. I didn't want to give an apology that wasn't one hundred percent genuine, and I didn't want to make hollow promises. I love you and I respect you, Bex. And I promise to always try to show you and anyone watching exactly how much I do."

Bex smiles that smile of hers that I love. "And I promise to always let you."

I laugh, and then just take in the look of joy on her face.

Bex licks some of the ice cream on her spoon, then studies the half that's left. "You know, you didn't have to go that public to show you want to be with me. Especially in front of *Business Success* magazine, or at an event that will be streaming to such a large audience of your fellow CEOs." She puts the spoon in her mouth, her eyes on me.

"No, that's exactly what I needed to do. I want them all to know. Bexlandians, too. I don't know if you noticed or not, but Nikki and Enoch were also there."

Her head jerks in surprise. "They were? Where?"

"Enoch was at the front, filming me, and Nikki was at the side, very discreetly filming you. So if you want to use any of the footage in a *Bexlandia* segment, it's all yours. I even give you my express permission to play me saying 'I was wrong' on a loop."

Bex laughs. "I might just have to do that."

"Wait. You lined this all up with my roommates so they would get me here and in that room, didn't you?"

I grin and take a bite of my ice cream. Then I set it aside and scoot in closer. She sets hers on the bench beside her, too, and turns to me. "And, Roman, I just want you to know that I am truly, madly, deeply, forever in love with every single part of you. From everything in here," she says, placing a hand on the side of my head, "right down to your fun socks."

"And you're okay with letting everyone know?"

She smiles and nods, grabbing hold of my shirt and pulling me in closer.

"Good. Because otherwise, that whole thing in there would be rather awkward."

"Uh-huh," she breathes against my lips. Then she kisses me, and nothing in my life has ever felt so right.

Epilogue

PEYTON

"Oh, my life, don't you just want that?" I motion from where I sit at the big table in the dining room to Bex and Roman, who are standing behind the island, making Rice Krispies treats with Bex's five-year-old nephew and three-year-old niece.

Timini looks up from the costume she's sketching a design for. "A Rice Krispies treat shaped like a stegosaurus? Sure."

"No, silly," I say. "The domestic bliss. Being a cute little family, hanging out in the kitchen together, making treats."

"Yeah," Addison says, glancing up from her computer, where she's probably online shopping for storage solutions for a client. "That looks nice."

Ian nods, too. Not in a *let's have a baby right now* way, but he is wearing an *I'd like that before long* expression.

I sigh as the five-year-old bumps into the three-year-old,

and she pushes back with her marshmallowy hand, sticking both her hand and some of her hair to her brother's shirt. Bex frees the hand and then helps the girl wash it before scooting their stools further apart and setting her on it again. All while Roman helps the five-year-old free a dinosaur from the cookie cutter he pressed into the treats. "Aren't they going to make the most adorable parents someday?"

"Totally," Timini says.

"Oh my lands, Bex, you could do a pregnancy segment on your channel! You could let your viewers go on the journey with you and talk about all the funny and weird and wild things that happen when you're pregnant."

"Whoa," Roman says, only taking his eyes off what his future nephew is doing for a small second to glance at me. "Let's not jump so far ahead yet. Right now, the wedding planning and the impossible task of finding a home is taking up every bit of time we have. Let's conquer those mountains first."

"Oh, speaking of which," Bex says, "your mom needs you to call her. Something about a long-lost uncle or someone who needs to be on the boutonnière list."

"But the wedding planning is going well?" I ask. I should be working on my schedule right now, planning out meals and grocery lists for my clients, but I have a hard time focusing on my notebook while all my roommates are in the same room as me.

"Yep!" Bex says as she helps her niece press little candy balls into the treats for the dinosaur's eyes. "Well, I mean, as well as they can go when you're planning a wedding big enough for my entire extended family and Roman's and his parents' considerable list of business associates."

"Go big or go home, right?" Roman smiles at Bex, and she grins back before they lean behind the kids and kiss.

The two of them are so freaking adorable, I can hardly stand it. I want someone to love as much as Bex and Roman or Ian and Addison love each other. I turn to Timini. "You're bringing someone to movie night, right?"

Timini lifts a shoulder in a shrug but doesn't stop sketching. "I think so. It's a first date with a guy named Jake… Jack…something like that. I mean, *if* he shows up. He seems a little flaky."

"If you, of all people, are calling someone flaky," Bex says, "I'm thinking the chance he'll show up isn't great."

Timini laughs, and then leans forward to grab an apple out of the bowl in the middle of the table and acts like she's going to throw it at Bex.

Bex's niece has a very concerned look on her face. "Does Timini not like you, Aunt Bex?"

"No, sweetie. Timini loves me."

"I do," Timini says to the little girl. "Even when she's probably right."

I don't have a date for movie night, so I asked my best friend, Max, to come. I glance at my watch. He planned to come a little early, which should be any minute. No sooner do I think it than I hear the unique sound his car makes as it pulls into the rounded driveway in front of the inn.

"Max is here!" I jump up and go to the front door, a skip in my step. I make it to the wrap-around porch just as he pulls to a stop, and I'm at the bottom of the three stairs just as he gets out of the car.

"I brought caramel popcorn," he says, holding the bag up.

"My favorite."

"I thought about getting a vegetable tray, but then I saw the popcorn and couldn't resist."

"You did not almost get a veggie tray."

He holds up a hand in surrender as we walk up the steps. "All right, you got me. I had a flashback to that one movie night when you tried to toss a carrot into my mouth and missed and hit me in the eye. I figured the popcorn was safer."

I give him a playful shove and then notice that the mailbox just beside the door has mail sticking up. Being the first person to notice always feels like I've won a scavenger hunt. I lift the flap, pull out the contents, and then scream.

Running into the house, Max right behind me—probably wondering what's happening—I shout, "Oh my stars, Bex! Roman! Everyone! It came!"

I race into the kitchen where everyone is standing, looking my way in alarm. There's no helping it, though—this is so exciting! I make a beeline to the table, and Bex and Roman quickly wash the sticky off their hands and rush around the island to crowd around the dining room table with everyone else.

I ceremoniously place the magazine right in the middle of the table so everyone can see. The glossy cover of *Business Success* magazine shows both Bex and Roman, both in business attire, giving each other the cutest *there's more to this story than you're seeing* looks on their faces. Bex's hand is on Roman's arm, and her engagement ring is absolutely shimmering in the studio lighting. The headline reads *These Two Executives Are Planning a Different Kind of Merger.*

"I think that's the prettiest magazine cover I've ever seen," Addison says.

Roman wraps an arm around Bex. She snuggles in close, then tips her head up and gives him a kiss on the lips.

I open the magazine to their article and read the subheading at the top out loud. "'After Roman Powell made the cover of our *Top 10 Young (and Single) CEOs* issue and, four months later, Bex Sterling was on our cover for the *Digital Content Creators to Keep Your Eye On* issue, we wanted to give you an update on these two executives, their rapidly growing businesses, and the joint venture they are about to embark on as they "tie the knot" on a merger that promises much future prosperity.' Aww! You two! This is so perfect!"

"We have to celebrate," Max says.

Bex looks at Roman, grinning. "Mandatory dance party in the family room?"

He grins back, and Bex gets out her phone to pull up her dance playlist as all of us head into the big gathering room. Within seconds, the music is on and booming and everyone is laughing and moving to the beat. Max is facing me, and we're both dancing like no one is watching. I love that he'll do things like have a spontaneous dance party without shying away. Everything Max does, he does with his full heart in it.

I add that to my mental list of what the perfect guy would be like. Really, what I want is someone exactly like

Max. (Minus the part of him that sees me like a sister, of course! Or the part where he doesn't seem to be interested in ever getting married and having kids, even though I think he'd be great at both.) But where do I even look to find someone that perfect? I've been searching for a while and just haven't found him.

My heart is full to bursting just being in this room with so many people I love, yet there's still something missing. I want that domestic bliss, and time cooking with kids, and sneaking kisses with the man I love so badly that my heart aches for it.

Do you know what? I've made up my mind. I'm going to come up with an out-of-the-box plan to find my perfect guy —no matter how ridiculous the plan has to be to work—and I'm going to find him soon.

———

Author's note:

I hope you loved Bex & Roman's story! And I hope you loved being back at Hidden Inn with Bex and her roommates. So far, two roommates have broken the pact, and Peyton is about to break it next. She is sweet, and so is her relationship with Max. And there are plenty of hijinks to be had in their story! (Especially with all their dates gone wrong.)(And the camping trip depicted on the cover.)

I hope it gives you exactly the kind of escape you need right now. Read on for a teeny sneak peek from the middle of one of Max's first chapters!

–Meg

———

"So, um, Peyton decided that she wants to get married."

Hunter's attention jerks to me. "To you?"

"Okay, you don't have to look so shocked. But no, genius, not to me. Just, in general, she's ready to get married."

"You kind of knew that already."

"True. But she's ready to speed up the process."

Peyton's my best friend—I want her to be happy. That doesn't mean I'm in love with the idea of her finding someone to spend her life with who isn't me. Imagining her married and moving forward with her life and leaving me behind has been playing over and over in my mind ever since she dropped that bomb on Sunday, and it's all making me a little crazy.

Hunter turns back to the screen, making adjustments to our design. "How is she planning to speed it up?"

I turn and lean against the design table, my arms folded. "A competition with me, actually. She wants us to see who can go on the highest number of dates—with a different person each time—in one week, and then we each take our favorite date to our friends Bex and Roman's wedding."

Hunter's still looking at the screen, but I can see the smile spreading across his face. "Stakes?"

"Karaoke for the loser."

This time, Hunter laughs. He even lets go of the mouse and turns in my direction so all his focus can be on me.

"And she wants us to be each other's wingman. So not only am I going to have to be hearing about her dates, but I'll actually be setting her up on dates with guys I know."

"Oh, man. I don't think you could get much more friend-zoned than that. Not that you haven't spent the last year pretty solidly in the friend zone."

"Thanks. I'm feeling better already."

Hunter chuckles. "Is she setting you up on dates as well?"

I nod.

"Well, at least you'll get a lot of dates out of the deal."

I let out a grunt of frustration and turn to the design screen. Getting a few dates isn't worth nearly as much as it's costing me.

Get *How to Not Fall for Your Best Friend* to read Peyton's and Max's story!

I have seven days and fifteen dates with different people to find my perfect guy—and to *not* fall for my best friend. Again.

Max Peyton is everything I want in a future husband: fun, kind, and just the right mix of responsible and adventurous. Plus, he's my best friend. He feels like comfort and acceptance and home, all wrapped into one.

But I absolutely *cannot* fall for him.

A year ago, when I almost (accidentally!) kissed him, he said he loved me like a sister. A *sister*. So, yeah, friend zone it is. Besides, Max doesn't want to get married to anyone. Ever. And I very much do.

Instead, I come up with a plan to find my perfect man. Max and I both need dates for a wedding, and I talk him into a competition to see which of us can go on the most dates, each with a different person, all within one week.

It's a brilliant plan, I'm sure of it. Seven days and we'll both have perfect wedding dates and be on our way to happily ever afters. My plan is practically foolproof.

Unless, of course, the only person I want to choose at the end… is him.

If you love best-friends-to-lovers, laugh-out-loud moments, and all the swoony feelings, you'll love How to Not Fall for Your Best Friend.

Start reading

Romancing the Spy

WANT TO READ MORE OF MEG'S ROMANTIC COMEDIES?

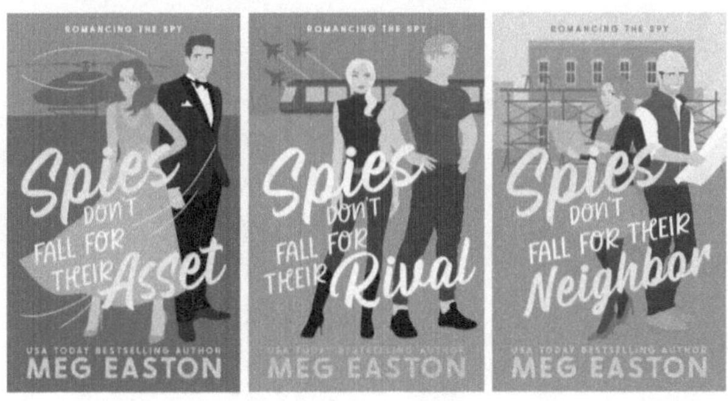

Need more adventure and humor in your life?

In a family where the spy business is the family business, falling in love is the real mission impossible. Follow the six Lancaster siblings—each uniquely trained, fiercely loyal, and more than a bit protective—as they navigate top-secret missions, unexpected romance, laugh-out-loud situations, witty banter, an abundance of chemistry, and lots of adventure.

Spies Don't Fall for Their Asset
Spies Don't Fall for Their Rival
Spies Don't Fall for Their Neighbor

Meg Easton is the *USA Today* bestselling author of contemporary romances and romantic comedies with fun, memorable, swoon-worthy characters, and settings you'll want to pack up and move to. She lives at the foot of a mountain with her name on it (or at least one letter of her name) in Utah. She loves gardening, bike riding, baking, swimming before the sun rises, and spending time with her husband and three kids.

She can be found online at www.megeaston.com

Sign up to receive her newsletter and stay up to date with new releases, get exclusive bonus content, and more.

If you liked this book please leave a review. Your review can help other readers find books they might fall in love with.

youtube.com/@megeastonauthor
bookbub.com/authors/meg-easton
instagram.com/megeaston_author
facebook.com/MegEastonBooks
tiktok.com/@megeaston_author